COMIC CHAPTER BOOKS

SCOOBY-DOO!

STONE ARCH BOOKS
a capstone imprint

Published in 2016 by Stone Arch Books,
A Capstone Imprint
1710 Roe Crest Drive,
North Mankato, Minnesota 56003
www.mycapstone.com

CAPS35805

Library of Congress Cataloging-in-Publication Data is
available on the Library of Congress website.

ISBN: 978-1-4965-3585-6 (library binding)
ISBN: 978-1-4965-3589-4 (paperback)
ISBN: 978-1-4965-3593-1 (eBook PDF)

Summary: Follow Scooby, Shaggy, Velma, Daphne, and
Fred into a bottomless cavern, which is haunted by the
ghosts of Civil War soldiers. Or is it? The Mystery Inc.
gang must uncover the secret of the haunted cave while
taking care of another bottomless pit:
Scooby's stomach!

Printed in the United States of America in North Mankato, Minnesota.
009660F16

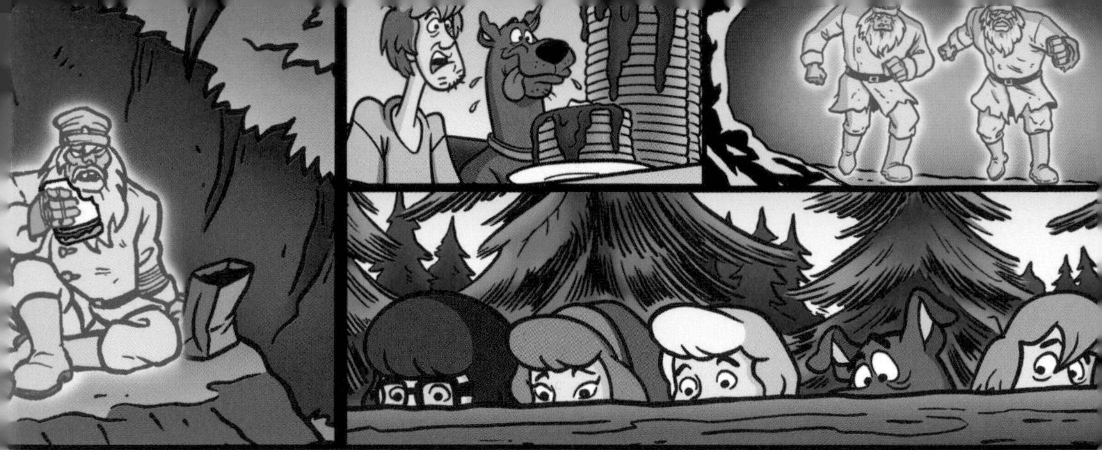

COMIC CHAPTER BOOKS

SCOOBY-DOO!™

written by Matthew K. Manning
illustrated by Scott Neely

SECRET OF THE HAUNTED CAVE

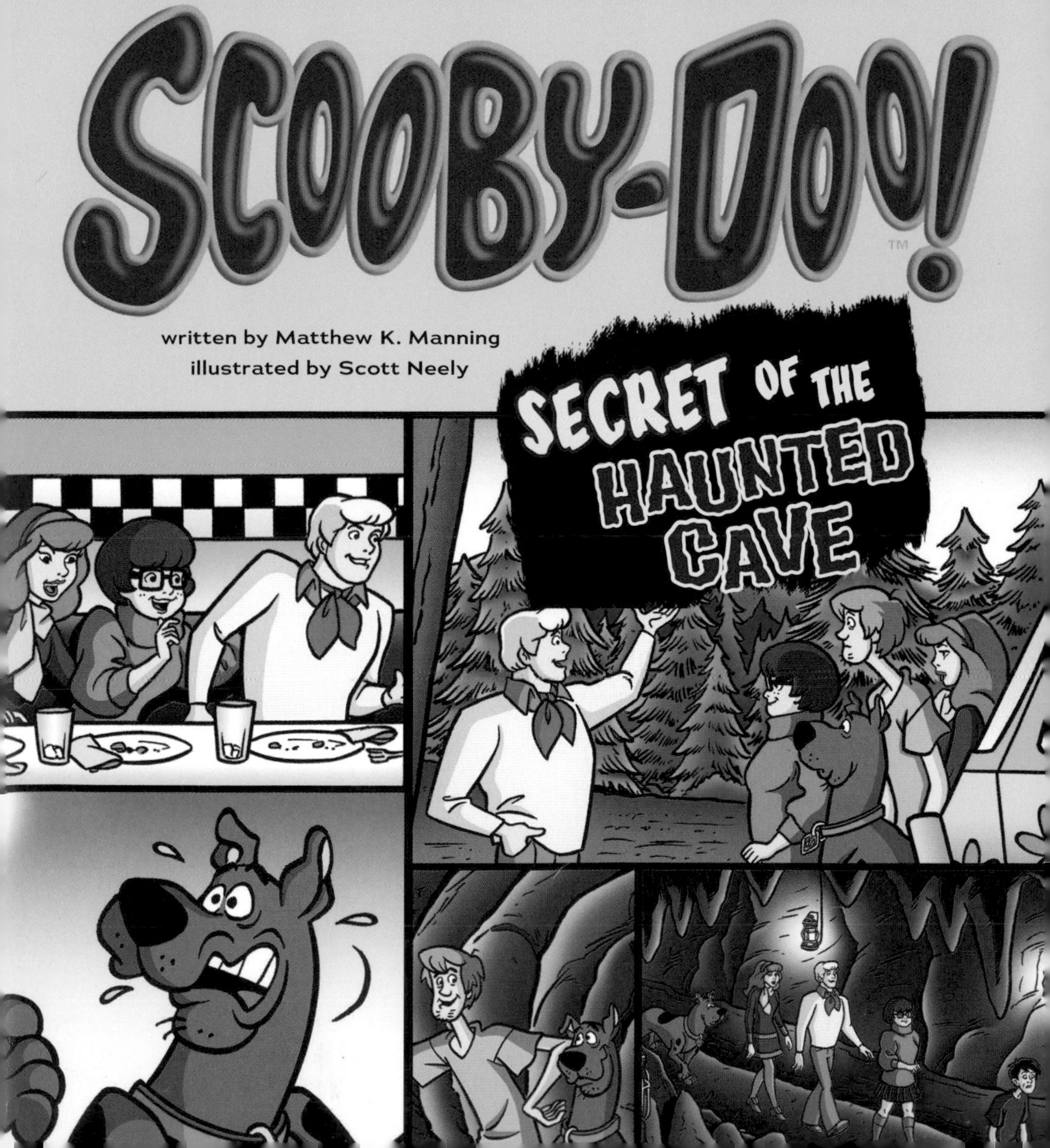

TABLE OF CONTENTS

MEET MYSTERY INC.

SCOOBY-DOO

SKILLS: LOYAL; SUPER SNOUT
BIO: THIS HAPPY-GO-LUCKY HOUND
AVOIDS SCARY SITUATIONS AT ALL
COSTS, BUT HE'LL DO ANYTHING FOR
A SCOOBY SNACK!

SHAGGY ROGERS

SKILLS: LUCKY; HEALTHY APPETITE
BIO: THIS LAID-BACK DUDE WOULD
RATHER LOOK FOR GRUB THAN
SEARCH FOR CLUES, BUT HE USUALLY
FINDS BOTH!

FRED JONES, JR.

SKILLS: ATHLETIC; CHARMING
BIO: THE LEADER AND OLDEST
MEMBER OF THE GANG. HE'S A GOOD
SPORT — AND GOOD AT THEM, TOO!

DAPHNE BLAKE

SKILLS: BRAINS; BEAUTY
BIO: AS A SIXTEEN-YEAR-OLD
FASHION QUEEN, DAPHNE SOLVES HER
MYSTERIES IN STYLE.

VELMA DINKLEY

SKILLS: CLEVER; HIGHLY INTELLIGENT
BIO: ALTHOUGH SHE'S THE YOUNGEST
MEMBER OF MYSTERY INC., VELMA'S AN
OLD PRO AT CATCHING CROOKS.

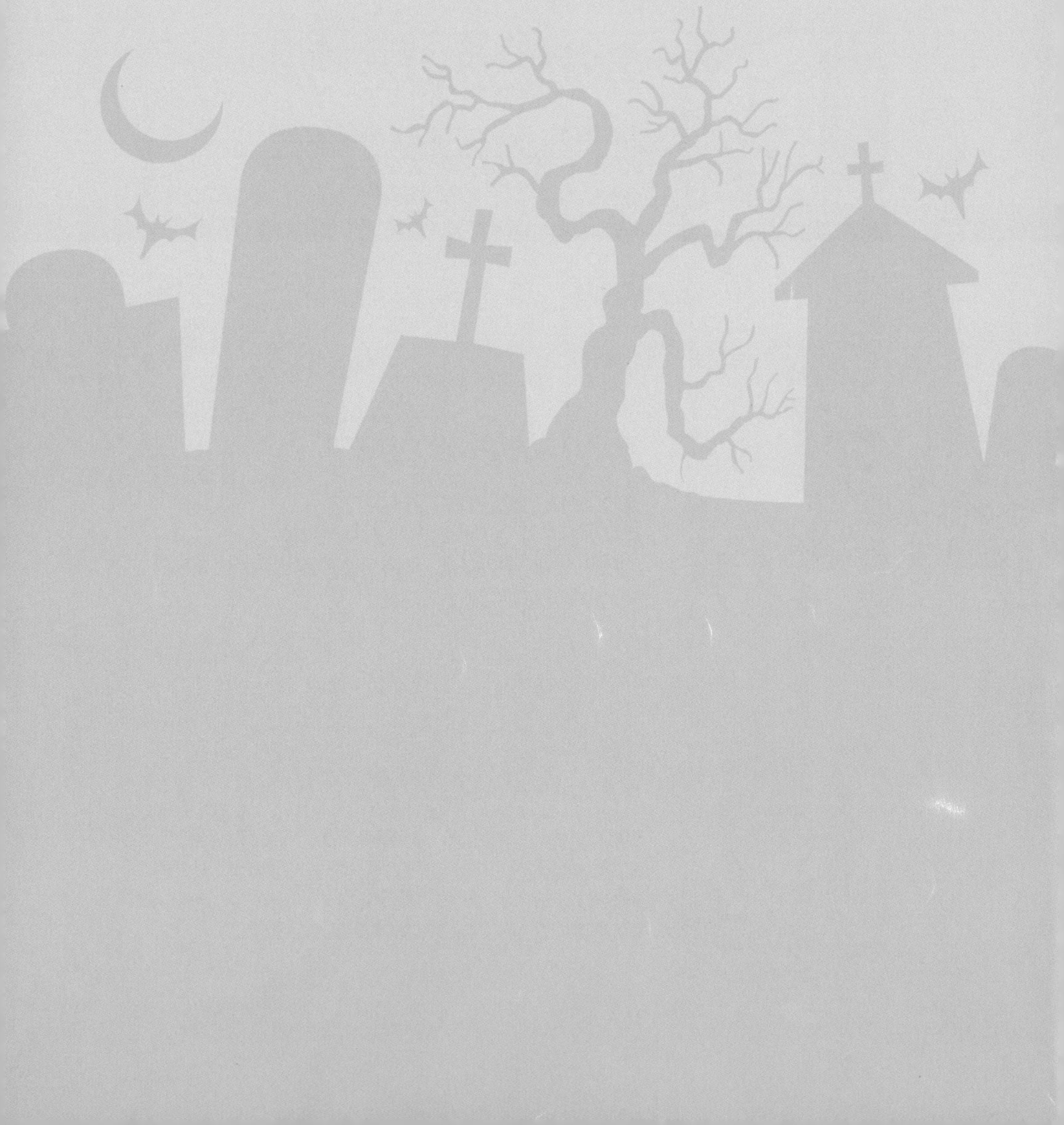

CHAPTER 1
WORD OF WARNING

SPLISH! SPLASH!

Large, slimy droplets pelted Shaggy's face. He awoke from a dream about parading hot dogs, hamburgers, and pizza slices.

"Like, is it raining in here?" he said, popping up in the backseat of the Mystery Machine.

SPLISH! SPLASH!

Shaggy wiped more slimy droplets from his forehead. Then he looked over at the seat beside him. "Scoobs!" he shouted.

Scooby-Doo was fast asleep. His head rested near the van's open window and his tongue flapped wildly in the breeze, sending spit flying like a garden sprinkler.

"Scoobs!" Shaggy shouted again.

"Ruh?" said Scooby-Doo, awakening suddenly. He'd been dreaming about a parade of ice-cream cones, candy bars, and apple pies.

"Like, I already showered today," joked Shaggy, wringing out the hem of his soaked green shirt.

"Rorry!" Scooby apologized.

SCREEEECH!

Just then, the van came to a sudden stop.

Shaggy stepped out the back doors of the Mystery Machine. He shielded his eyes from the sun and began to sweat. The weather was unseasonably hot for western North Carolina.

Shaggy already missed the blue and green van's air conditioning. "Like, sheesh!" he said. "Who left the oven on?"

His loyal dog Scooby-Doo followed him out of the van. The Great Dane squinted up at the bright sun. Scooby-Doo immediately jumped back inside the Mystery Machine.

"Come on, Scooby," said Velma. "It's not that bad." She had already walked around the side of the van. Velma always insisted on riding in the front seat. It was like she wanted to know what was happening before anyone else.

"It'll be cool in the cave," said Fred. He was rounding the other side of the Mystery Machine.

On long trips like these, Fred was always found behind the wheel. If Velma wanted to be the first to know what was going on, Fred wanted to be right there with her.

"Well then let's go in there already," said Shaggy.

"Fred's right," said Velma. "Many of the spiders and crickets found in caverns rely on a cool climate to survive."

"Riders rand rickets?" said Scooby-Doo, peeking his head out of the back of the van.

"Let's never go in there already!" Shaggy insisted.

Scooby ducked back in the Mystery Machine.

"Well, if Scooby's staying in the van, the four of us will have to eat at that delicious-smelling diner without him," said Daphne.

Daphne jumped out of the back of the van and stretched. She'd taken a short nap while the Mystery Inc. gang had wound through the nearby mountains for the last hour or so.

"Riner?" Scooby popped his head out of the van again.

"Like, why didn't you say so?!" Shaggy exclaimed. Before the gang could say anything else, he and Scooby were already halfway to the smaller of the two buildings that connected to the parking lot.

"That was easy," Daphne said. She closed the van's back doors.

"They're kind of predictable that way," said Velma.

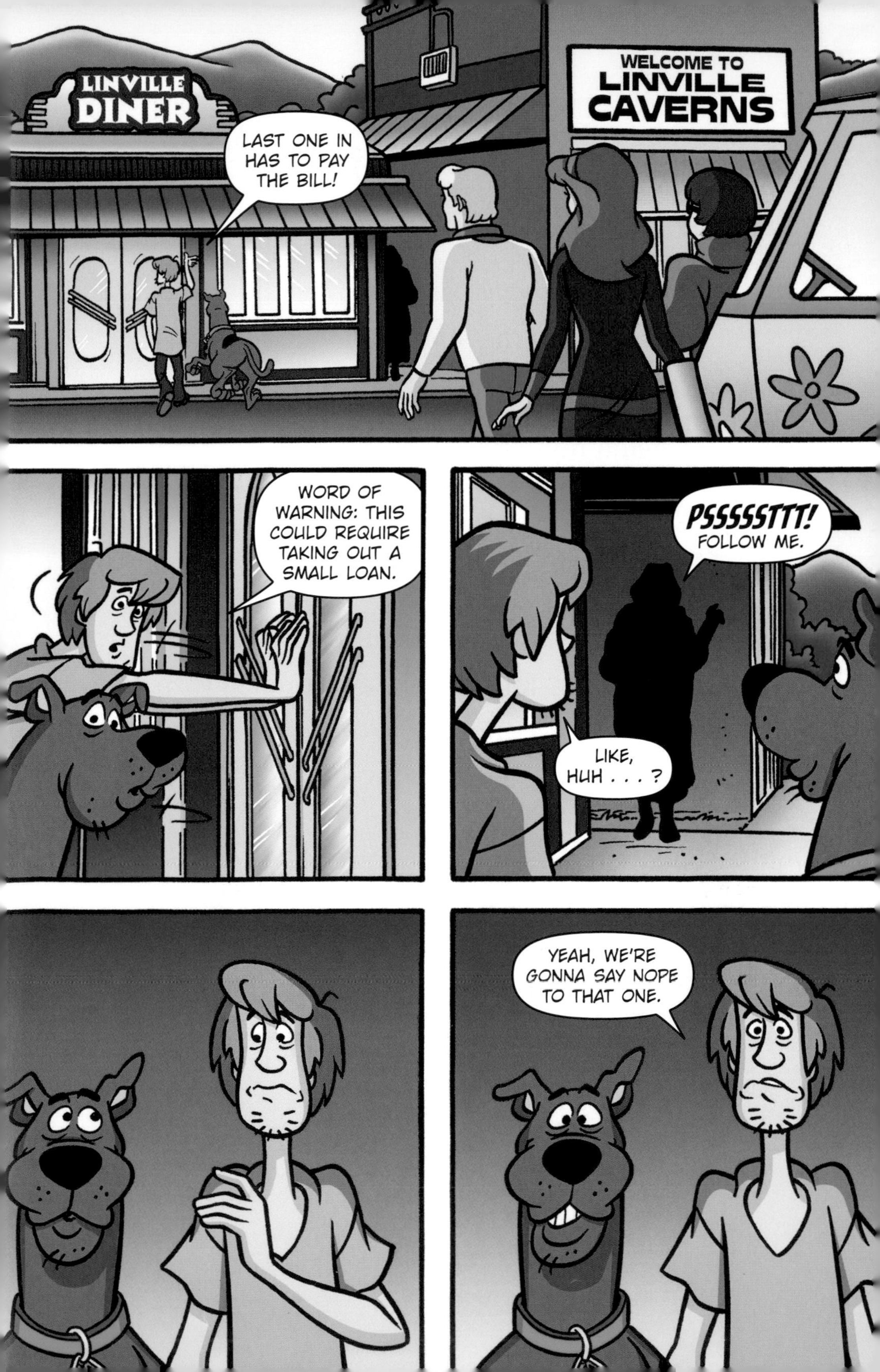
LINVILLE DINER
WELCOME TO LINVILLE CAVERNS
LAST ONE IN HAS TO PAY THE BILL!
WORD OF WARNING: THIS COULD REQUIRE TAKING OUT A SMALL LOAN.
PSSSSSTTT! FOLLOW ME.
LIKE, HUH . . . ?
YEAH, WE'RE GONNA SAY NOPE TO THAT ONE.

"What was that all about?" asked Daphne as she, Fred, and Velma caught up with Shaggy and Scooby-Doo.

"Like, some creepy person wanted us to follow her behind the diner," Shaggy said. "We respectfully declined."

"I smell a mystery!" said Fred.

"Well, I smell french fries," said Shaggy.

SNIFF! SNIFF!

Scooby-Doo sniffed at the air with his sensitive snout. "Ruh-uh!" Scooby argued with Shaggy. "Ronions rings!"

SNIFF! SNIFF!

Shaggy smelled the air again. "Like, we'll have to agree to disagree," he said.

But it was too late to argue. Fred, Velma, and Daphne were already rounding the corner of the diner.

"Ah, man!" said Shaggy. "Tell me again why we hang out with those guys?"

"Scooby Snacks," Scooby said.

"That's a pretty good argument," said Shaggy.

The alley between the two buildings wasn't as spooky as Shaggy and Scooby had feared. In fact, with the shade from the sun, it seemed like a nice little place for an unplanned picnic.

A dark figure standing at the end of the alley didn't seem quite as inviting. "Come closer," the figure said. From the sound of her voice, Shaggy could instantly tell it was a woman. "I have something to tell you," she said.

Fred gathered his courage and took the lead. Daphne and Velma weren't far behind.

"Um, okay," Fred said.

Fred took a step forward, and so did the mysterious woman. Out of the shadows, it was clear that she was covered in a thick, blanket-like coat with a hood that hid her hair.

"Don't go in the cave," she said through mostly missing teeth.

"Why not?" Velma asked.

"There are spirits there," the woman warned. "Unfriendly spirits trapped in a world they no longer understand."

"Sounds like us at that science fair Velma dragged us to," Shaggy said to Scooby.

Scooby-Doo wasn't listening to his old friend. He was focused on the mysterious old woman and her warning.

"There is something unnatural in there," said the woman. She was also doing a fairly decent job of ignoring Shaggy. "Some who have entered have never returned."

"What about the diner?" said Shaggy. "Same deal there? Or do people survive the cheeseburger and fries?"

Scooby-Doo licked his chops.

The old woman gave a nearly toothless grin. "I used to laugh at the unexplained, too," she said, looking at Shaggy. He smiled, but he couldn't help but shiver.

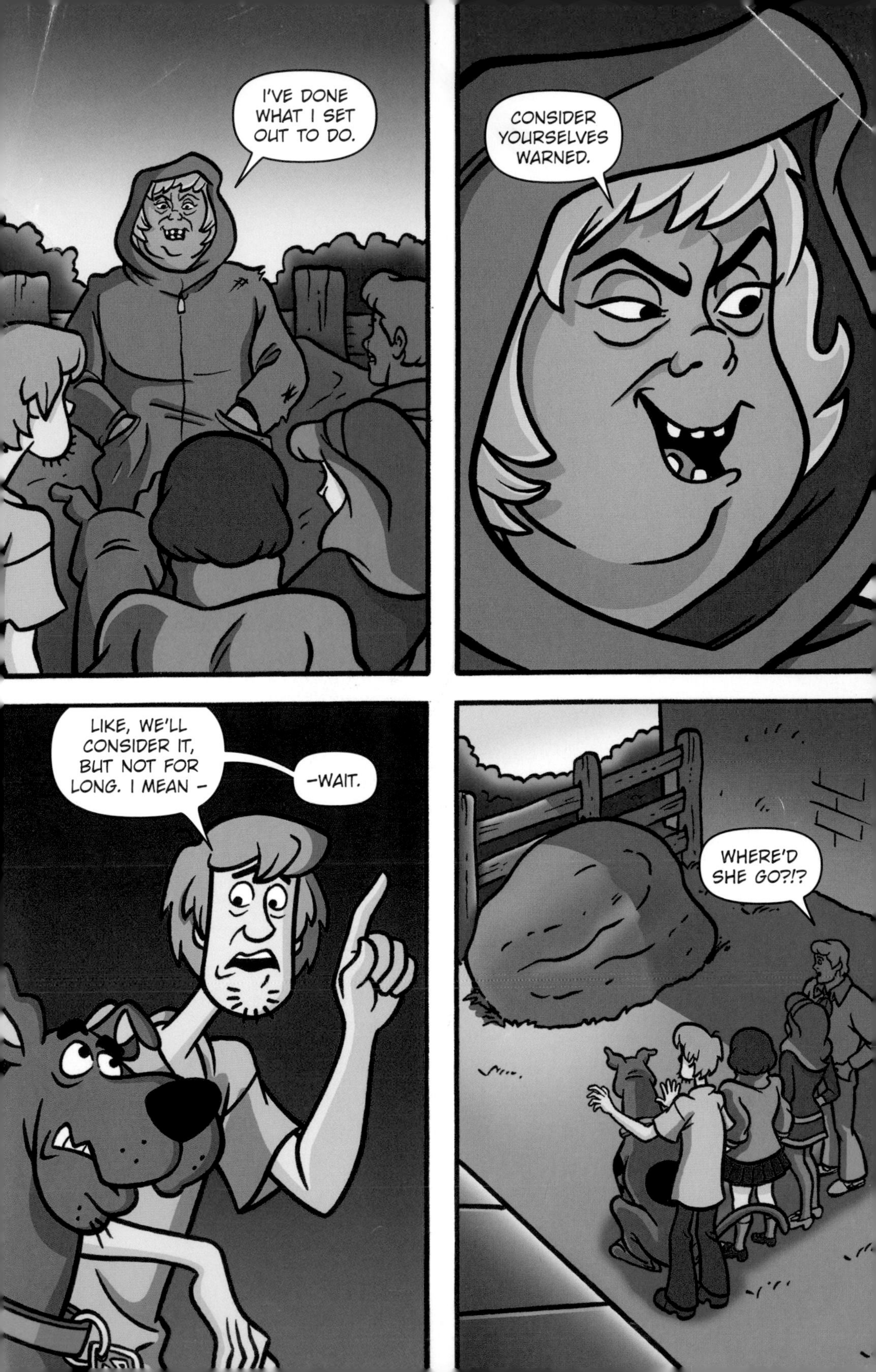
I'VE DONE WHAT I SET OUT TO DO.
CONSIDER YOURSELVES WARNED.
LIKE, WE'LL CONSIDER IT, BUT NOT FOR LONG. I MEAN –
–WAIT.
WHERE'D SHE GO?!?

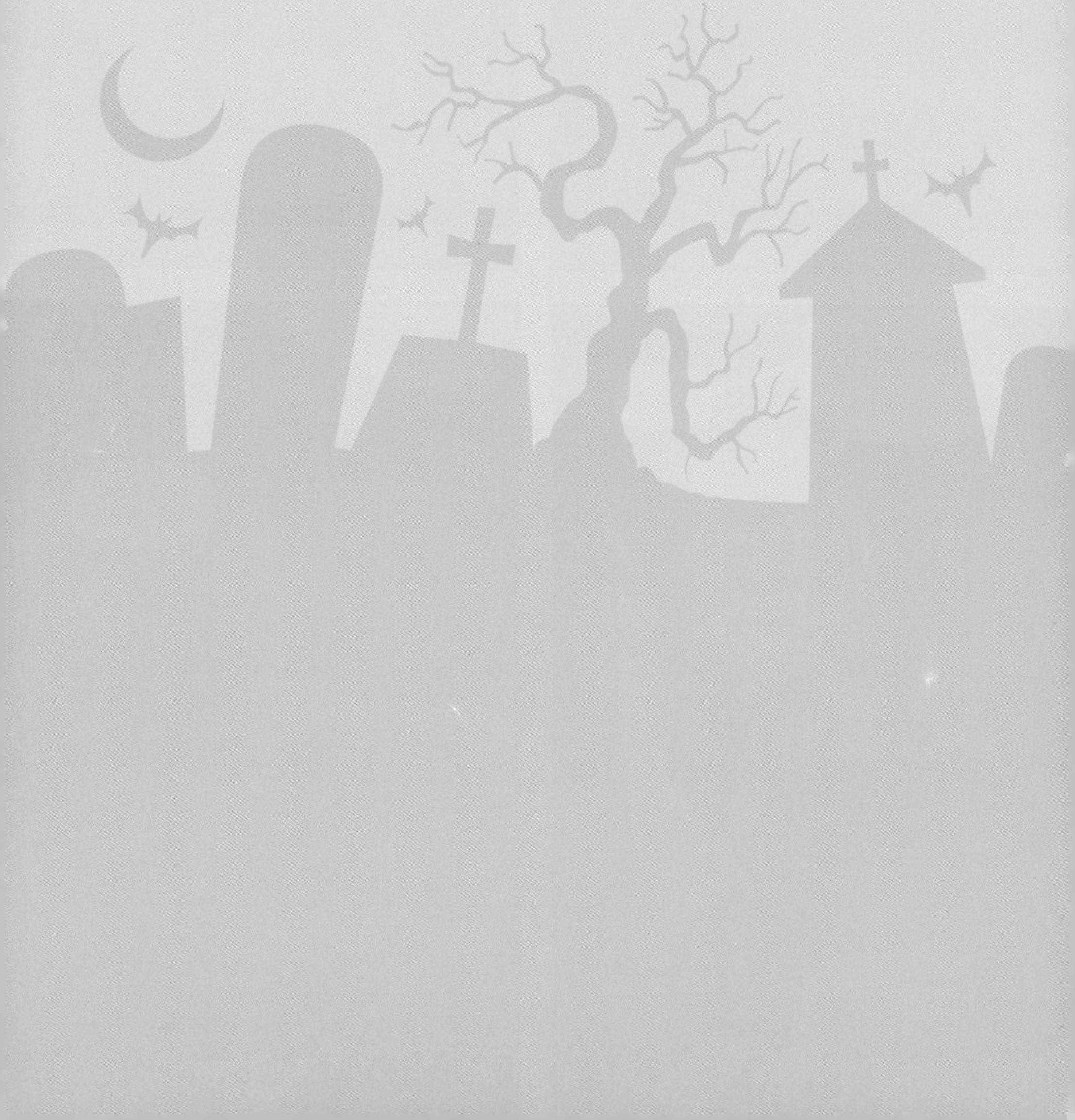

CHAPTER 2
A HEAPING HELPING OF MYSTERY

MUNCH! MUNCH! MUNCH!

Inside the diner, an exhausted waiter placed another tray of pancake stacks in front of Scooby-Doo and Shaggy.

Scooby drizzled a pitcher full of maple syrup over the entire tray. Then the hungry hound stuck his fork through one of the stacks and swallowed all ten pancakes and one gulp.

"Rummy!" he said, quickly digging his fork into another stack.

MUNCH! MUNCH! MUNCH!

"Like, save some for me, Scoobs!" cried Shaggy as he finished off a plate of breakfast sausages and bacon.

Talking to Scooby-Doo and Shaggy over the mountains of pancakes piled in front of them was nearly impossible. Daphne put in her best effort, anyway.

"Are you guys done yet?" she asked from her side of the booth inside the diner.

"Ha!" said Shaggy, peering around his pancake stack. "You and your sense of humor, Daph." He looked over to Scooby who shared the padded booth's bench with him. "Did you hear her, Scoobs? Are we done yet? Isn't she a riot!"

"Reah!" said Scooby. "Ra riot!" Scooby-Doo finished off the final stack of pancakes and then flagged down the waiter. "Rwo rore," he said.

The waiter wiped sweat from his brow. "Only two more pancakes?" he asked, sounding relieved.

Shaggy laughed. "Like, he means two more trays of pancakes," he explained.

The waiter hung his head and headed back into the kitchen.

Daphne sighed and slumped back in her seat. Next to her, Fred and Velma were having their own conversation.

"So what kind of spirits do you think we're dealing with?" asked Fred.

"Odds are, it's the phony kind," Velma replied. "That woman wasn't exactly the definition of a credible witness."

"A credible what now?" came a booming voice from behind the gang's table. "You folks in the law game?"

"Hardly," said Fred as he turned around to face a man in a pink shirt and pink tie. He was an imposing figure. He wasn't exactly tall, but he had broad shoulders and a large face. His chin seemed to disappear into his neck, and his combed-over hair could have used a trim a few years ago.

"We're in the mystery game," said Velma, turning to smile at the stranger.

"Not many winners in that," said the man.

"You'd be surprised," said Daphne, joining the conversation. After all, anything was better than watching Scooby and Shaggy devour what had to be North Carolina's entire supply of pancakes.

"Name's Wellcott," said the man. "John B. to my friends."

"Nice to meet you," said Velma. She and the gang introduced themselves, even if Scooby and Shaggy were a bit hard for Mr. Wellcott to understand. Their mouths were too full to carry on much of a conversation.

"So it's a mystery that's brought you out to Linville Caverns?" Mr. Wellcott asked.

"More like a mystery found us after we got here," said Velma.

"The ghosts, huh?" Mr. Wellcott said. "Yeah, well, it is a shame, at that."

"Have you seen them?" asked Fred. "What kind of ghosts are we talking about?"

"I'd be lying if I said I hadn't," said Wellcott. "There's not many around these parts who haven't seen 'em. Poor souls, trapped in that cave. We should just leave 'em alone, if you want my honest opinion."

"Can you give us any details?" asked Velma. "Anything at all would help our investigation."

"I think there's been enough talk of nonsense around here for today," came another voice. Velma and the rest of the gang turned their heads to see a tall, slender man approach their table. It wasn't hard to guess his occupation. He was clearly the local sheriff. The badge and hat he wore were a dead giveaway. "Let's go, Wellcott. Leave the tourists alone, huh?"

"Don't pretend that you ain't seen 'em, Jeremiah," said Mr. Wellcott. "He's seen 'em just like the rest of us." He turned back to the gang. "These folks deserve a warning before they waste money on admission to that cursed cave."

With that, Wellcott straightened his back and adjusted his tie. He nodded to the gang and gave the sheriff a dirty look.

"Just keep walking," said the sheriff. He turned back to the gang. "That's the trouble with the idle rich," he said. "They've got nothing to do but idle."

"No problem at all," said Fred. "We happen to like a good ghost story."

"Well if it's nonsense you want, you came to the right place," he said. "Personally, I don't see the value of much here except for Suzy's key lime pie."

"So you've never seen the ghost of the caverns for yourself?" Daphne asked.

The sheriff looked at her and tightened his mouth. After what seemed easily like a good two minutes, the sheriff finally spoke. "Have a nice day." He tipped his hat at Daphne and then turned and walked out of the diner.

"So that was weird," Daphne said.

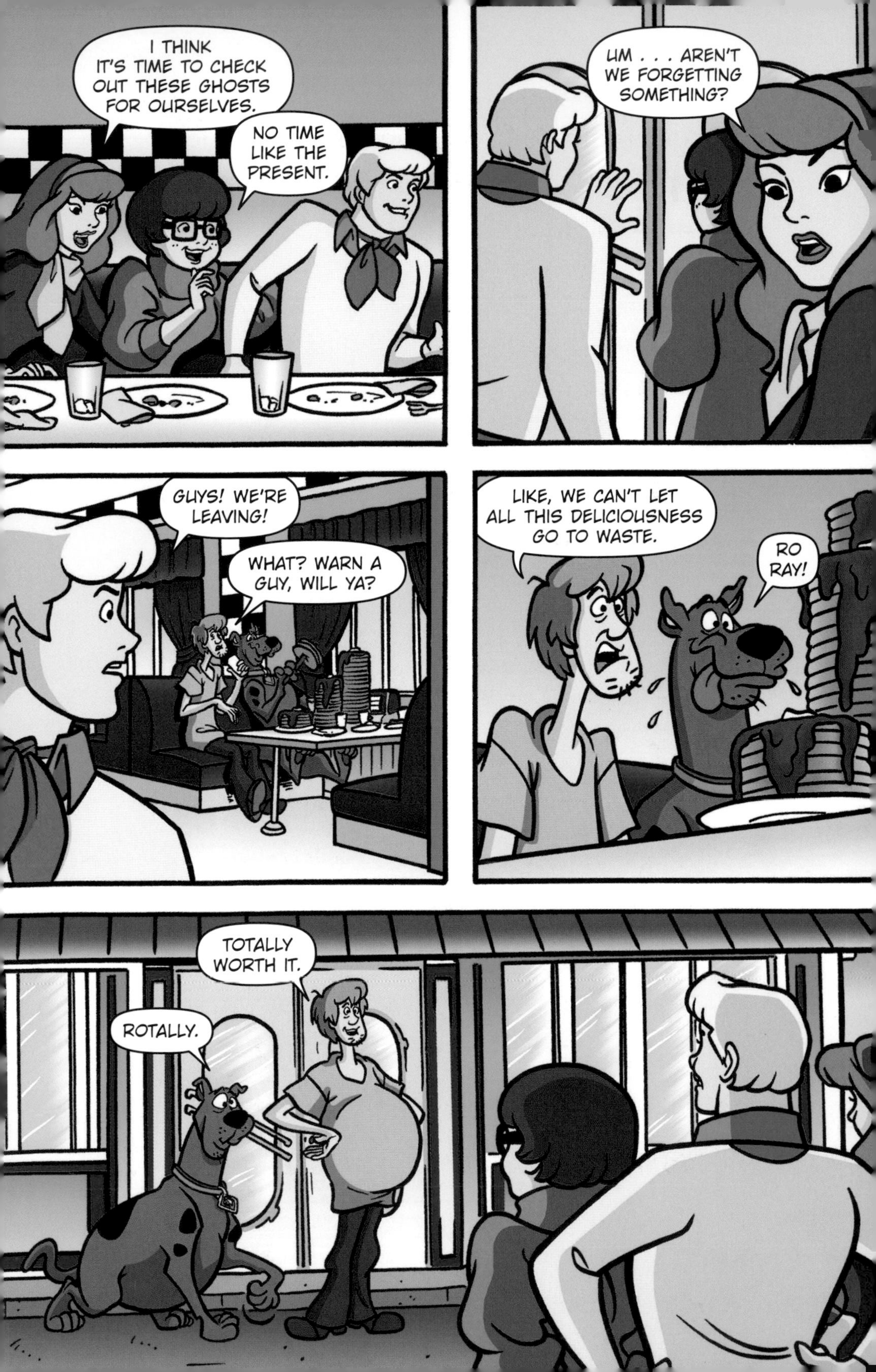
I THINK IT'S TIME TO CHECK OUT THESE GHOSTS FOR OURSELVES.
NO TIME LIKE THE PRESENT.
UM . . . AREN'T WE FORGETTING SOMETHING?
GUYS! WE'RE LEAVING!
WHAT? WARN A GUY, WILL YA?
LIKE, WE CAN'T LET ALL THIS DELICIOUSNESS GO TO WASTE.
RO RAY!
TOTALLY WORTH IT.
ROTALLY.

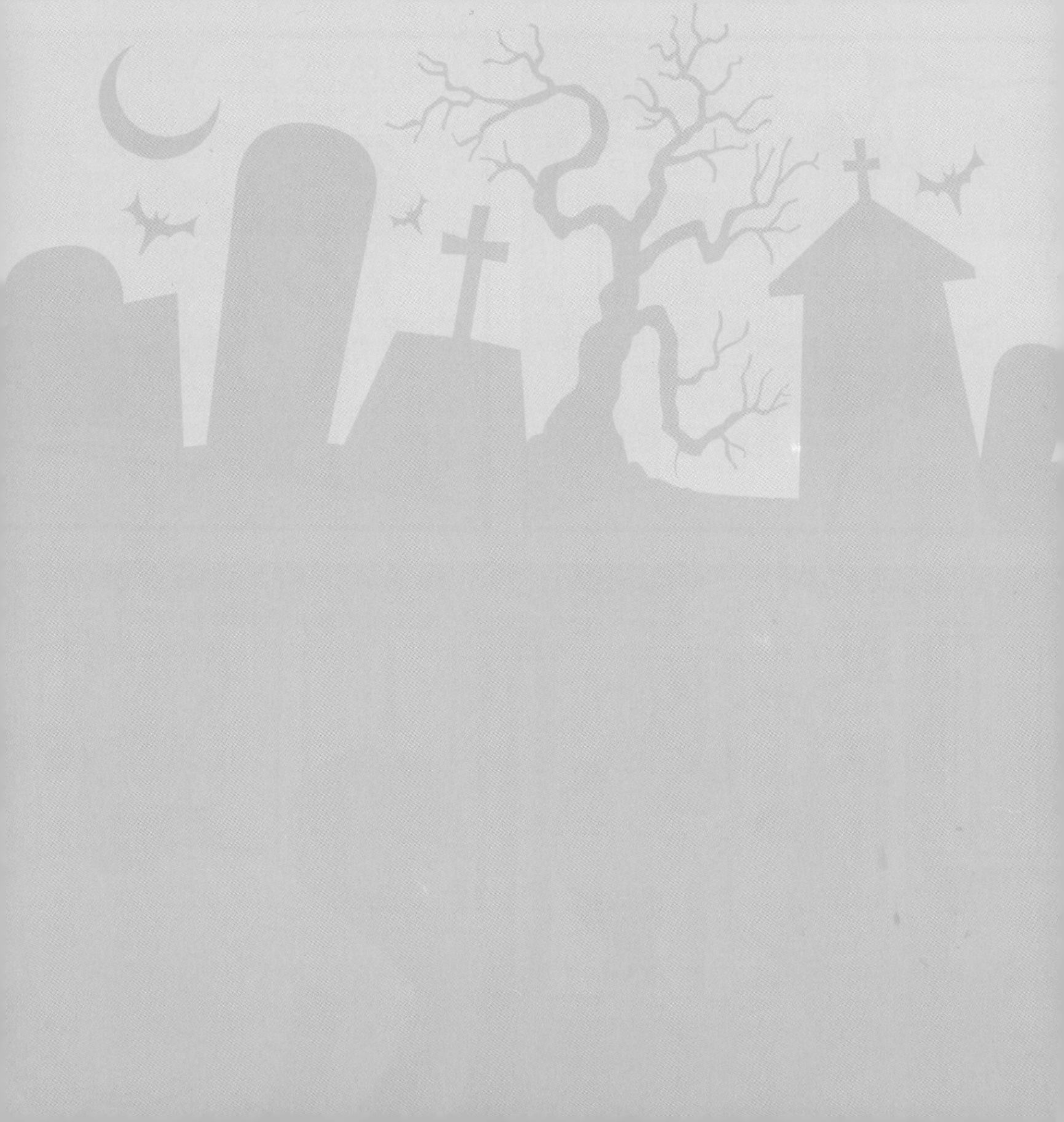

CHAPTER 3

"Simon!" shouted the woman behind the gift shop counter. "Simon! Get out here. We have customers."

The head of a teenager with messy black hair and large eyes popped up above a display of souvenir license plates. "Huh?" he said, sounding surprised. Apparently customers weren't a common thing at the shop.

It didn't take much detection on the gang's part to conclude that this young man was indeed Simon.

"I've been calling for like a half hour," said the brown-haired woman behind the counter. She wore thick-rimmed glasses that couldn't hide the angry look in her eyes.

"Sorry," said Simon. He walked over to the counter where the Mystery Inc. gang stood. They had just purchased their tickets for the cave tour. It seemed Simon would be their rather unwilling guide.

"Follow me," he said in something barely louder than a whisper. The gang all exchanged glances. Then they did what Simon had asked. "Cave entrance is this way."

He led them down a concrete ramp and around a corner. At the end of the sidewalk was a large metal door installed right in the side of the mountain.

"Worked off those pancakes, yet?" Velma asked Scooby and Shaggy as the gang stepped inside the cave.

A loud grumbling sound suddenly echoed off the cave's rocky walls.

GRUMMMBLLLLLEE

"Like what was that?" Shaggy cried out. He quickly hid behind Scooby-Doo.

As usual, the pair lagged a few paces behind the rest of the gang.

GRUMMMBLLLLLEE

Scooby held his grumbling stomach. "Rorry!" he barked.

"Don't be sorry," Shaggy said. "I'll take an angry stomach over a polite ghost any day!"

Scooby smiled at Shaggy, but it wasn't very convincing. He was so stuffed, all he could think about doing was finding a shady spot and taking a quick catnap. Or dog nap, as it were.

"Feast your eyes on the wonders you're about to behold," Simon muttered. "This cave system was first discovered more than two hundred years ago," he said as he pulled the metal door open. "Although this particular entrance is only about a decade old, the caves were considered sacred by natives of western North Carolina."

SOLDIERS HID IN THESE VERY CAVES DURING THE CIVIL WAR.

THEY USED THE UNDERWATER STREAMS AS A SOURCE OF CLEAN WATER.

IT'S SAID THAT MANY SOLDIERS WERE NEVER DISCOVERED.

WHAT BECAME OF THEM HAS BEEN LOST TO ANTIQUE . . . ANTIQUITY . . .

UM, LOST TO HISTORY.

WHAT WERE WE WORRIED ABOUT, SCOOB? THIS PLACE ISN'T HALF AS FREAKY AS WE THOUGHT.

WALK THIS WAY, BUT DO NOT TOUCH THE CAVE'S WALLS. IT COULD DAMAGE THE SURFACE OR DISTURB THE SPIDERS.

GULP

SPIDERS?!

RESUME WORRYING! RESUME WORRYING!

The tour had just turned a corner when Scooby and Shaggy caught up to them. Simon had stopped the group to talk about the narrow corridor they were walking through.

WHAM!

Scooby and Shaggy ran smack into Daphne when they found her. Luckily, Daphne managed to keep her balance. If she'd fallen, she would have knocked over Fred, and started a chain reaction of human dominos.

"Whoa!" Daphne exclaimed. "Watch it, guys!"

"Rorry," said Scooby.

"Like, what he said," Shaggy added.

"Ahem," grunted Simon. He wasn't used to having his tours interrupted. He also wasn't sure he really cared one way or the other.

When everyone was looking in his direction again, he began his poorly rehearsed speech. "On your left, if you look over the railing," he said, "you'll see the bottomless pit of doom."

Simon lacked so much energy that he may as well have been describing the inside of his refrigerator.

"Bottomless?" said Velma. "Really?"

"No one knows how far down it goes," said Simon. "It filled with water years ago, and it's too narrow for divers." He cleared his voice and then pointed to a different tunnel up ahead. "If you'll follow me, we'll head to the innermost chamber of the cave."

The gang shuffled forward down the narrow passageway. Velma stayed behind for a moment, though. She looked down over the railing at the black water below. She stared at her reflection, wondering just how deep the pit actually went.

Suddenly, her reflection's eyes began to twinkle. Then the light got brighter, as if there was a greenish white light glowing beneath the water's surface. Velma took off her glasses, wiped them, and then put them back on.

The light was gone.

"Jinkies," she said quietly to herself. She felt the hairs on the back of her neck stand up. Then she hurried on to find her friends.

***

"What you're about to experience, few people have ever seen," Simon was saying when Velma caught back up to the group. He waved his arms above his head for dramatic effect. It looked like he was trying to signal a plane to come in for a landing. "Only in the ocean's greatest depths can one witness the event about to unfold right in front of your very faces."

"What a delivery," Daphne whispered to Fred. He smirked and looked back at Velma. She faked a smile, but Fred could tell something was bothering her.

"I will now turn off the lights, so you may see this wonder for yourselves," said Simon. "Behold," he continued, "absolute darkness."

He reached for the light switch installed in the cave wall next to him. He attempted to flip it without looking and missed.

Simon smiled an awkward grin. "Um, behold," he said again, "absolute darkness."

This time he managed to flip the switch. Or at least, Fred assumed he did. It was impossible to see anything at the moment. The gang was far enough inside the cave that there was absolutely no light penetrating the chamber.

"Like, whoa!" came a familiar voice in front of Fred.

"Reah!" came another voice. "Rhoa!"

CLICK-CLACK! CLICK-CLACK!

A loud chattering sound suddenly filled the darkened cave. "Do you hear that, Scoobs?" Shaggy asked his canine friend.

"Ruh-huh!" Scooby confirmed.

CLICK-CLACK! CLICK-CLACK!

"Like, there it is again!" Shaggy cried out. "The old lady was right — this cave is cursed!"

"Scooby? Would you like a Scooby Snack?" Velma asked, shaking a small box of Scooby's favorite snack.

"Ripee!" Scooby-Doo exclaimed and then sniffed his way to the treats.

CHOMP! CHOMP! CHOMP!

The chattering teeth sound quickly turned into a chomping sound.

"One mystery solved," said Velma.

"And another one begins," came Daphne's voice through the darkness. "It doesn't look like absolute darkness to me."

"Sheesh!" said Shaggy. "How dark do you want it to get?"

"Look up ahead," said Daphne. "See! There's some kind of light."

The rest of the Mystery Inc. gang hadn't noticed it, but sure enough, Daphne was right.

There was some sort of faint glow coming from down a tunnel behind Simon.

"What is that? Sunlight?" Fred asked.

"No, Fred," said Daphne. "It's getting closer!"

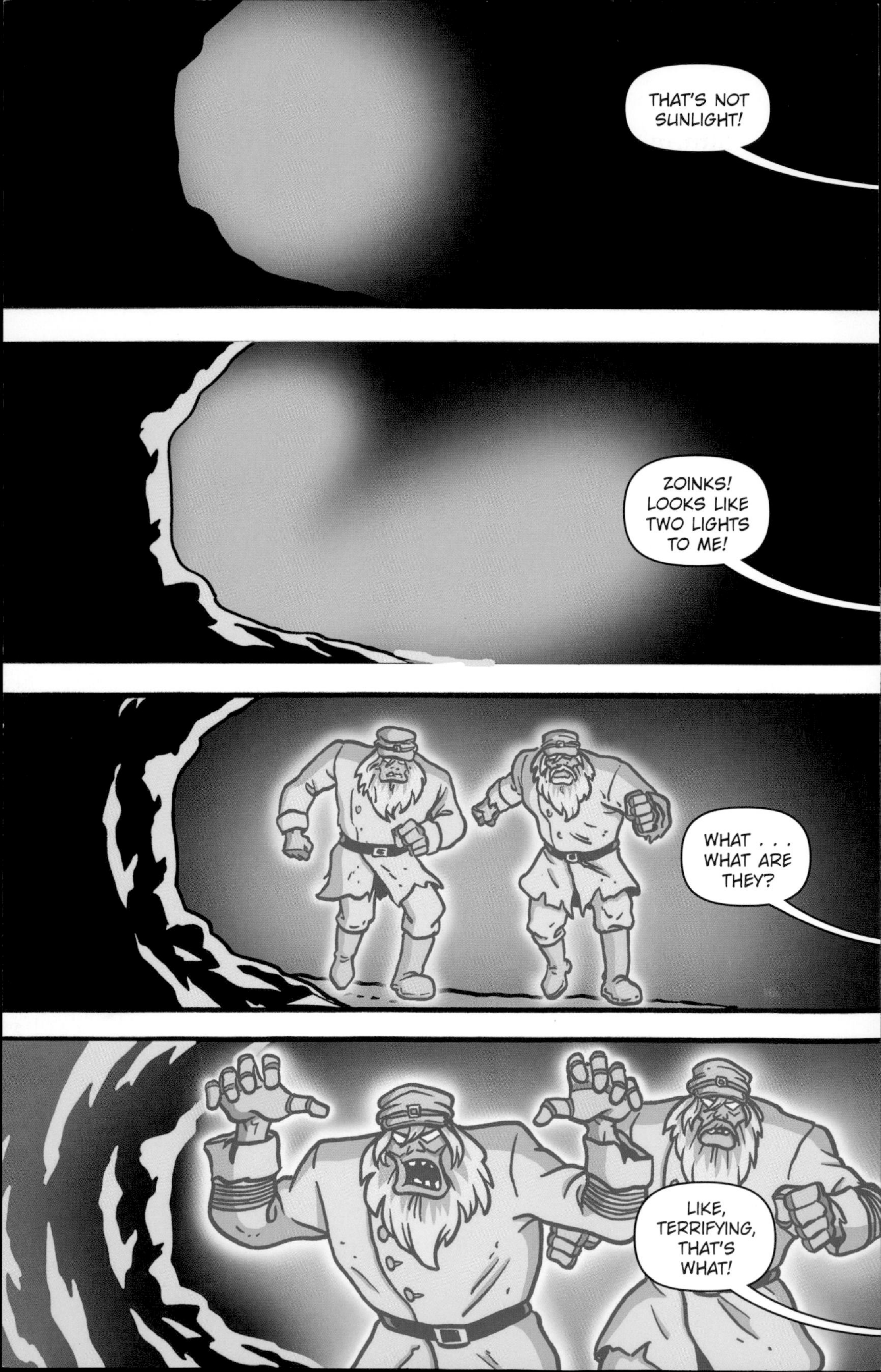
THAT'S NOT SUNLIGHT!
ZOINKS! LOOKS LIKE TWO LIGHTS TO ME!
WHAT . . . WHAT ARE THEY?
LIKE, TERRIFYING, THAT'S WHAT!

Simon hadn't seen the strange glowing men yet. They were behind him, and he had been focusing his attention elsewhere. He had been fumbling for the light switch for the last full minute. When he finally did flip the switch, he felt extremely proud of himself. That feeling didn't last very long.

"Like, behind you!" Shaggy shouted.

Simon turned around and saw the two glowing soldiers coming toward him. "Um," he said, "the next tour isn't for another hour."

"I don't think those are paid guests," Daphne said.

"Why aren't we running yet?" Shaggy yelled as the ghosts came closer. The gang looked at each other for a split second and then took Shaggy's suggestion. But just as they did, the lights turned off again.

"This way!" Fred yelled.

The problem was, none of them could see where they were going. In fact, the only thing they knew was the direction not to head in.

All they could see in the darkness were the two fast-approaching ghost soldiers.

Fred felt someone grab his arm. He tried to shake it off, until he heard Daphne speak. "It's me," she said.

"It's who?" said Simon. He had managed to keep up as the gang rushed down the closest tunnel.

"Who's that?" said Daphne. "Is that the guide?"

Simon didn't answer. He had made the mistake of looking back over his shoulder as the trio shuffled quickly forward. He could see one of the ghost soldiers hot on their heels.

"Simon," said Fred as he continued to lead Daphne down one of the cave's pathways. "Is that you?"

"Uh-huh," Simon said. "Hey, I think that thing may be a ghost."

"Wow," said Fred. "Thanks for the heads-up."

"Any idea where we're going?" asked Daphne.

"She's talking to you, Simon," said Fred.

Simon had turned around again. The ghost was getting closer. Simon could tell by its expression that it wasn't the friendly type.

"Simon!" yelled Fred as he bumped into the wall in front of him. He was feeling his way as fast as he could, but it wasn't easy. The cave had more than its share of twists and turns. "We could use a little help!"

Simon had frozen in his tracks. The young tour guide had been working for the Linville Caverns for only a few days. This was his first encounter with the ghosts he'd heard so much about. He thought for a moment that he much preferred the darkness to the glowing figure that was fast approaching him.

Simon simply shut his eyes and hoped for the best.

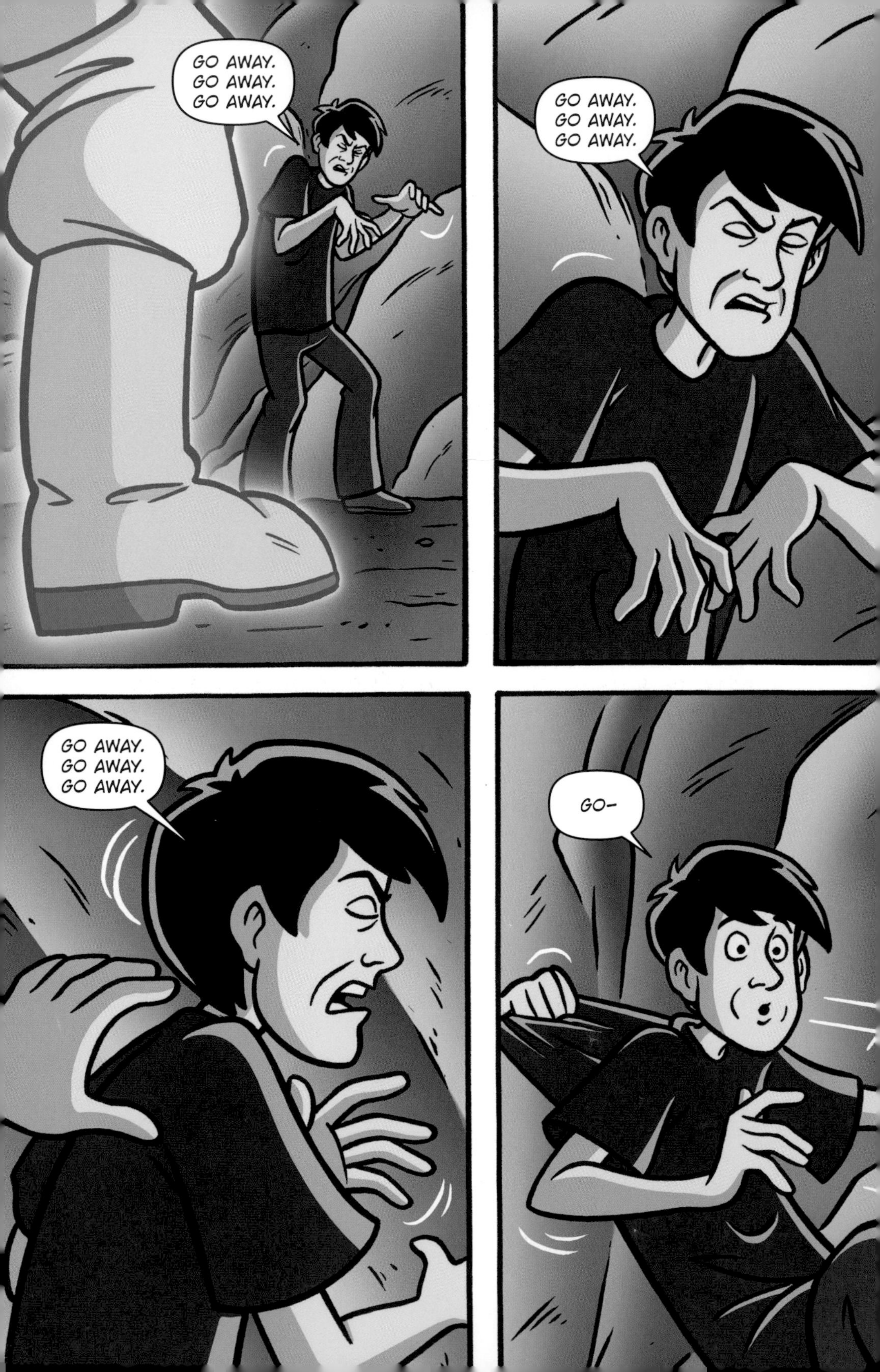
GO AWAY.
GO AWAY.
GO AWAY.
GO AWAY.
GO AWAY.
GO AWAY.
GO AWAY.
GO AWAY.
GO AWAY.
GO-

***

Shaggy thought it was a good sign when they got far enough away from the ghost that they couldn't see it any longer. Of course, now they couldn't see anything else, either!

He and Scooby weren't sure what tunnel they had made their escape through. All they cared about at the time was getting away from the glowing ghost soldiers. Looking back on it, Shaggy wished he had thought out his escape plan a little better. Wherever they were walking now, he was positive it wasn't one of the tunnels on the tour.

"R-r-rold," said Scooby. He shivered as he spoke. Shaggy couldn't see the shiver, but he could certainly hear it in his friend's voice.

"Me, too, Scoobs," he said. "Probably has something to do with this puddle of water we're standing in." The pair had been walking through that "puddle" for the last five minutes. Shaggy hadn't really given it much notice. But after saying it out loud, he realized that no puddle was that big.

"Hey, you think we're walking through that underground creek we saw earlier?" asked Shaggy. "The one that ran by the main path?"

"Reah!" Scooby said. He nodded his head, but Shaggy would never know it.

"Good thing it's not too deep," said Shaggy. "I wouldn't want to get wetter than —"

It was hard to hear the rest of Shaggy's sentence. The sound of splashing drowned it out.

"Hey!" said a familiar voice.

"Velma?" said Shaggy. "Like, is that you?"

"Shaggy?" Velma answered.

"Rand Scooby!" added Scooby-Doo.

"Am I glad to run into you two," said Velma.

"I don't know. Are you?" Shaggy asked. He and Velma couldn't see each other, but they were both now sitting in the six inches of water in the cave's underground creek. They had run directly into one another, but at least they were together again.

"Help me find my glasses," Velma said. She moved her hand through the water around her.

"Here they are!" said Shaggy.

He picked up the frames from his lap and held them out to her. Velma fumbled, but she managed to take them from him and put them back on. Unfortunately for her, they didn't make her jet black surroundings look any less jet black.

"So how do we get out of here?" asked Shaggy.

"Let me think for a second," said Velma. She started to stand up, but paused in midmotion. She felt the water again with her hands. "That's it!"

"If you're pointing to something, I have no idea what it is," said Shaggy. "Like, maybe try words?"

"The water in this creek," said Velma. "I remember it was flowing toward us when we entered the cave. We just need to follow the water, and it'll lead us to an exit."

"Renius!" Scooby exclaimed.

"Yeah, great thinking, Velma!" said Shaggy. He stood up and put his hand on her shoulder. "Lead the way!"

Velma began to shuffle forward. Her two friends splashed along behind her.

* * *

Fred hadn't exactly dragged Simon behind him as he ran through the cave, but it had been close. The young tour guide didn't seem to have the best survival instincts. When a ghost of a Civil War soldier charged at him, he simply shut his eyes, hoping it would go away. If Fred hadn't pulled Simon out of harm's way, he might have never seen the young teen again.

To be technical, Fred still hadn't actually seen Simon since that moment. The cave was still too dark to see much of anything. But he had certainly heard Simon the whole way down the tunnel. The tour guide's mouth hadn't stopped running, even if his legs didn't work quite as well.

"So that was a ghost?" Simon was asking. "Like a real ghost? Like the kind you hear about on TV?"

"Simon," whispered Daphne, "you need to be quiet now."

"You ever notice how you really never see ghosts on television?" Simon said. "You know, on those ghost-hunting shows? No one ever sees a ghost. They don't get it on tape. You just hear scratching on a recorder or something. It's really kind of —"

"Simon," whispered Fred. His whisper was a lot harsher than Daphne's. "Be quiet! We're trying to lose that guy, remember?"

"Oh," said Simon, as if finally realizing the situation. "Um, sorry?"

Fred, Daphne, and their confused tagalong had been running through various random tunnels for quite some time. Even if it wasn't so dark, Fred doubted he'd be able to find his way back to the others. They'd gotten themselves completely lost inside the cave system.

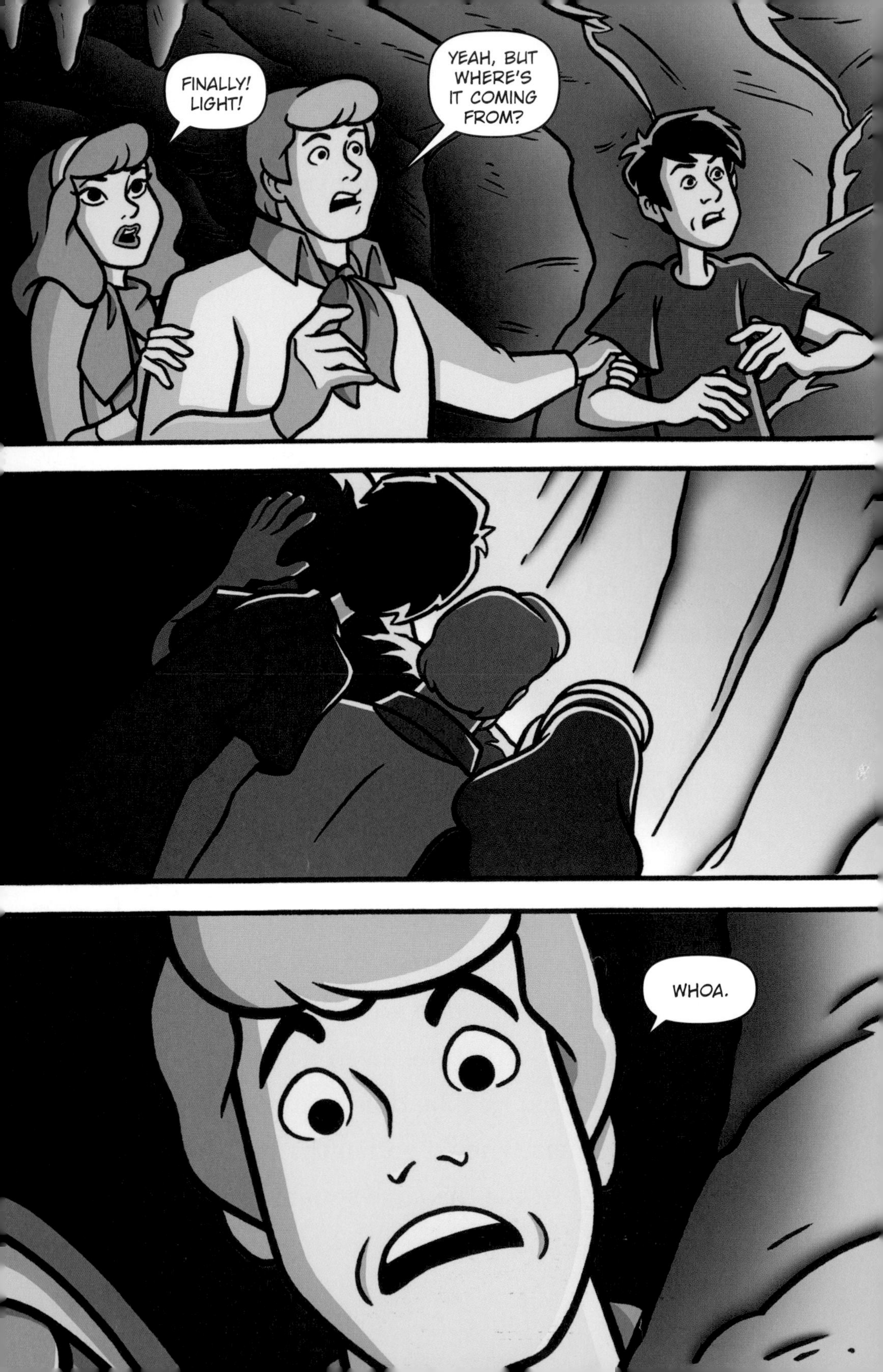
FINALLY! LIGHT!
YEAH, BUT WHERE'S IT COMING FROM?
WHOA.

Fred couldn't believe what he was seeing. The cavern in front of him was massive. There was a large pool at its center. It was something like an underground lake. But that wasn't the strange part. The pond was a greenish white light. It was like nothing he'd ever seen before. And the smell was absolutely terrible.

Daphne put her hand on Fred's shoulder. "You hear that?" she said. Fred hadn't at first, but now there was no denying it. Some voices were echoing through the large chamber. It sounded like they were getting closer.

Fred, Daphne, and Simon ducked back around the corner of the cave wall. "What is that stuff?" Daphne whispered.

"I don't know," said Fred. "I wonder if it has any connection to those spirits we saw earlier."

As if in reply to Fred's question, Simon made a slight whimpering sound. Fred and Daphne looked over to him, only to see both Civil War soldier ghosts standing next to them. The ghosts were smiling.

"Run!" Fred yelled. It no longer seemed like a priority to whisper.

Fred, Daphne, and a terrified Simon shot back down the dark tunnel from which they had come. They moved quickly, even as the light around them began to fade. The tunnel in front of them branched off in three directions. Fred bit his bottom lip and then chose the middle path. Daphne and Simon followed, hoping that Fred had more of a plan than they did. But as they ran into another jet black tunnel, they realized he was just making it up as he went along.

Fred stopped abruptly. Daphne and Simon did their best not to collide into their leader. It was a pretty difficult exercise.

"They're not following," Fred said between gasps for air.

"How do you know?" asked Simon.

"They glow, just like that cavern," said Fred. "We'd see them coming pretty easily in this darkness."

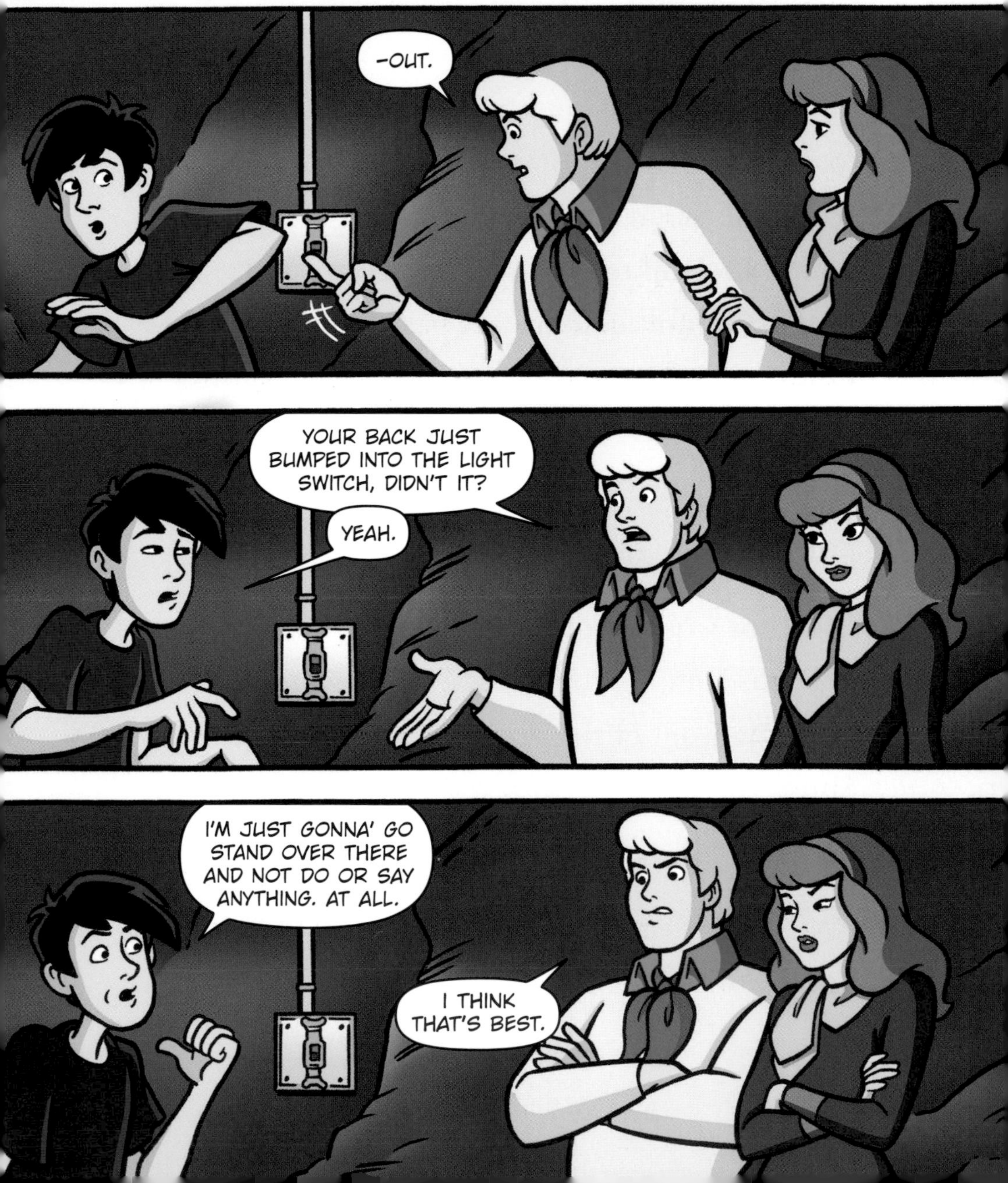

-OUT.
YOUR BACK JUST BUMPED INTO THE LIGHT SWITCH, DIDN'T IT?
YEAH.
I'M JUST GONNA' GO STAND OVER THERE AND NOT DO OR SAY ANYTHING. AT ALL.
I THINK THAT'S BEST.

Fred looked at the cave wall behind Simon. The rather unhelpful tour guide had accidentally leaned against the same light switch he'd turned off earlier. The group was back where they started. Luckily for them, the ghosts were still nowhere in sight.

With the lights to guide their way, it didn't take long for the trio to reach the front exit to cave. As soon as they were back in daylight, Simon took off toward the gift shop. Fred imagined him diving back behind a display of knickknacks, hiding from any and all future cave tours.

Daphne squinted in the light of the hot sun. "What now?" she said.

"That was our question, too," said Velma. She was walking toward Fred and Daphne from near the front of the diner. Scooby-Doo and Shaggy were sitting at a picnic table in the sun, drying themselves as best they could.

"What happened to you guys?" Daphne said as she noticed Velma's soaking wet skirt.

"Just a little impromptu cave swimming," Velma said.

Fred and Velma locked eyes. It was like they were talking to each other, but not saying a thing. "I think it's best we go," said Fred.

"Like, finally!" said Shaggy. "I was beginning to think that Scooby and I were the only people with any sense around here."

CHAPTER 4

HAZARDOUS SITUATION

The Mystery Machine's engine revved and then took off with a **SQUEEEEEEEAL!**

"Like, what's the rush, Fred?" Shaggy asked from the backseat. "Are you in a hurry to get back home?

"We're not heading home," Fred called back to him from the driver's seat.

"Zoinks!" Shaggy exclaimed

"Rouble roinks," added Scooby-Doo, who was sitting next to him.

"Scooby and I really are the only people with any sense around here," said Shaggy in disbelief.

"Oh come on, Shaggy," said Velma. "Where's your sense of adventure?"

"I think I left it somewhere back on the cave floor when those two ghost soldiers scared it right out of me," said Shaggy.

He looked over at Scooby-Doo who was also seated on the van's shag carpet. Scooby gave Shaggy a sympathetic smile. This wasn't his idea of fun, either.

The attitude in the front of the Mystery Machine was a different story. Fred, Daphne, and Velma were all excited to be driving through the North Carolina mountains on back roads that people probably hadn't driven on in decades.

"So tell me again why we're doing what we're doing," said Shaggy.

"We're looking for a back entrance," said Daphne.

"Yeah, you heard Simon," added Velma. "He mentioned that the cave's front door had been built only about ten years ago. So if there really were soldiers hiding out in the cavern during the Civil War, that means there has to be another way in."

"And I think we're there," said Fred as he pulled the van off the side of the road. The Mystery Machine came to a stop. Fred turned off the ignition. "That mountain has to be the back side of the cave system."

"Perfect!" Velma said. She opened the passenger door to the van and jumped out.

"Nuh-uh," said Shaggy, shaking his head. "I'm not going."

"Re reither," Scooby barked.

Velma shook her box of treats again. "Not even for a Scooby Snack?" she asked.

Scooby-Doo and Shaggy both licked their lips. They quickly hopped out of the van without another word. It had been a while since breakfast, after all.

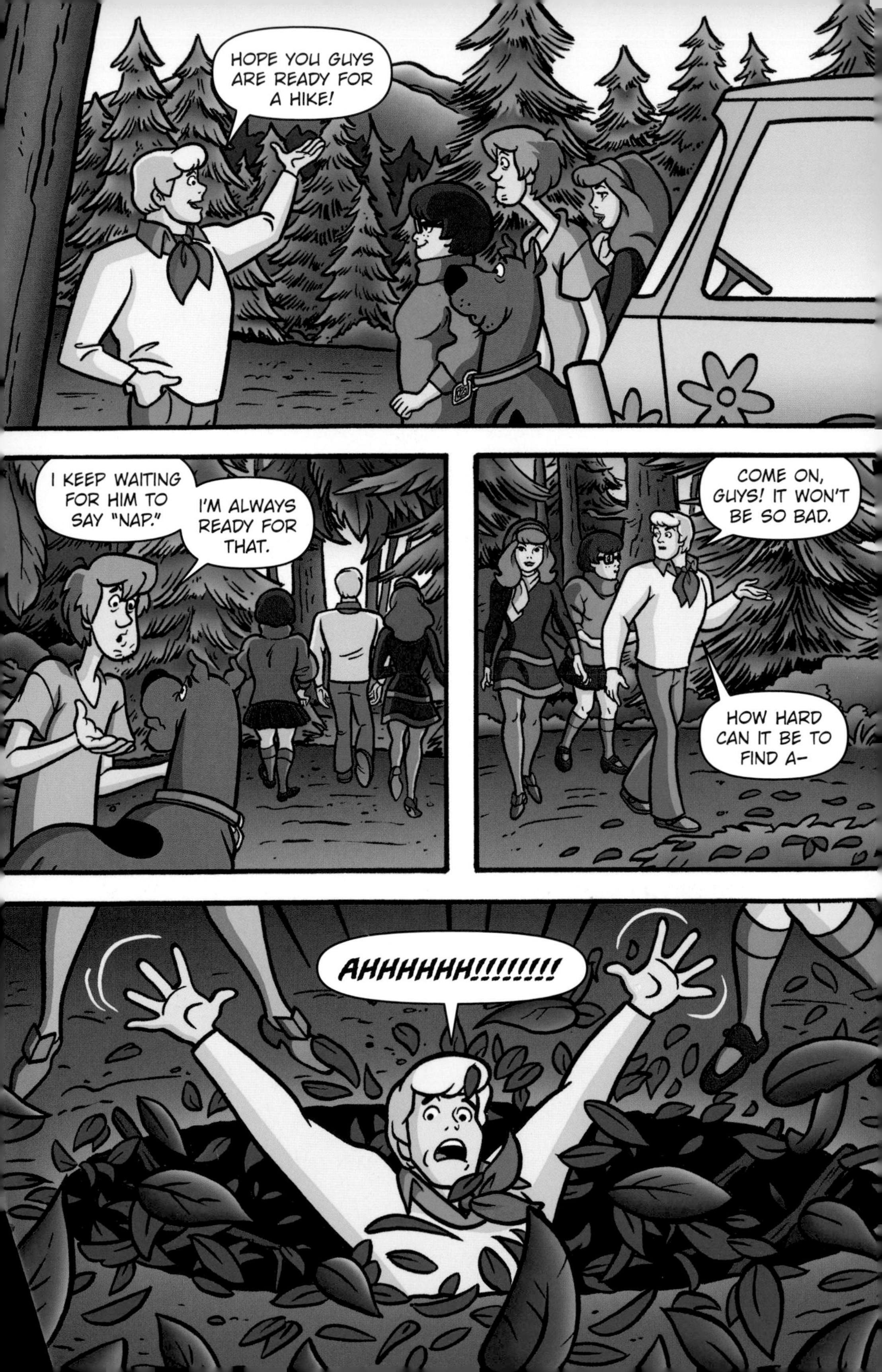
HOPE YOU GUYS ARE READY FOR A HIKE!
I KEEP WAITING FOR HIM TO SAY "NAP."
I'M ALWAYS READY FOR THAT.
COME ON, GUYS! IT WON'T BE SO BAD.
HOW HARD CAN IT BE TO FIND A–
AHHHHHH!!!!!!!!

"There must be dozens of holes like this, strewn around this side of the mountain," said Velma, looking down at Fred.

"I'm just happy it wasn't that deep," said Fred as he finished pushing himself back onto the surface. He hadn't fallen far. The hole he'd discovered in the ground was barely taller than him. With the help of a nearby root and a good jump, Fred had no problem boosting himself right back out again.

"So now can we go?" said Shaggy. "We found another way in. That was the goal, right?"

"But this is obviously not the entrance our 'ghosts' are using," said Fred. "It was completely covered up. You could probably get to the rest of the cave system from there, but no one has used that way for years . . . if ever."

"They're ghosts," said Shaggy. "Since when did ghosts need an entrance, anyway?"

"These do," said Daphne. She was hurrying down the hill toward her friends. "You guys may want to see this."

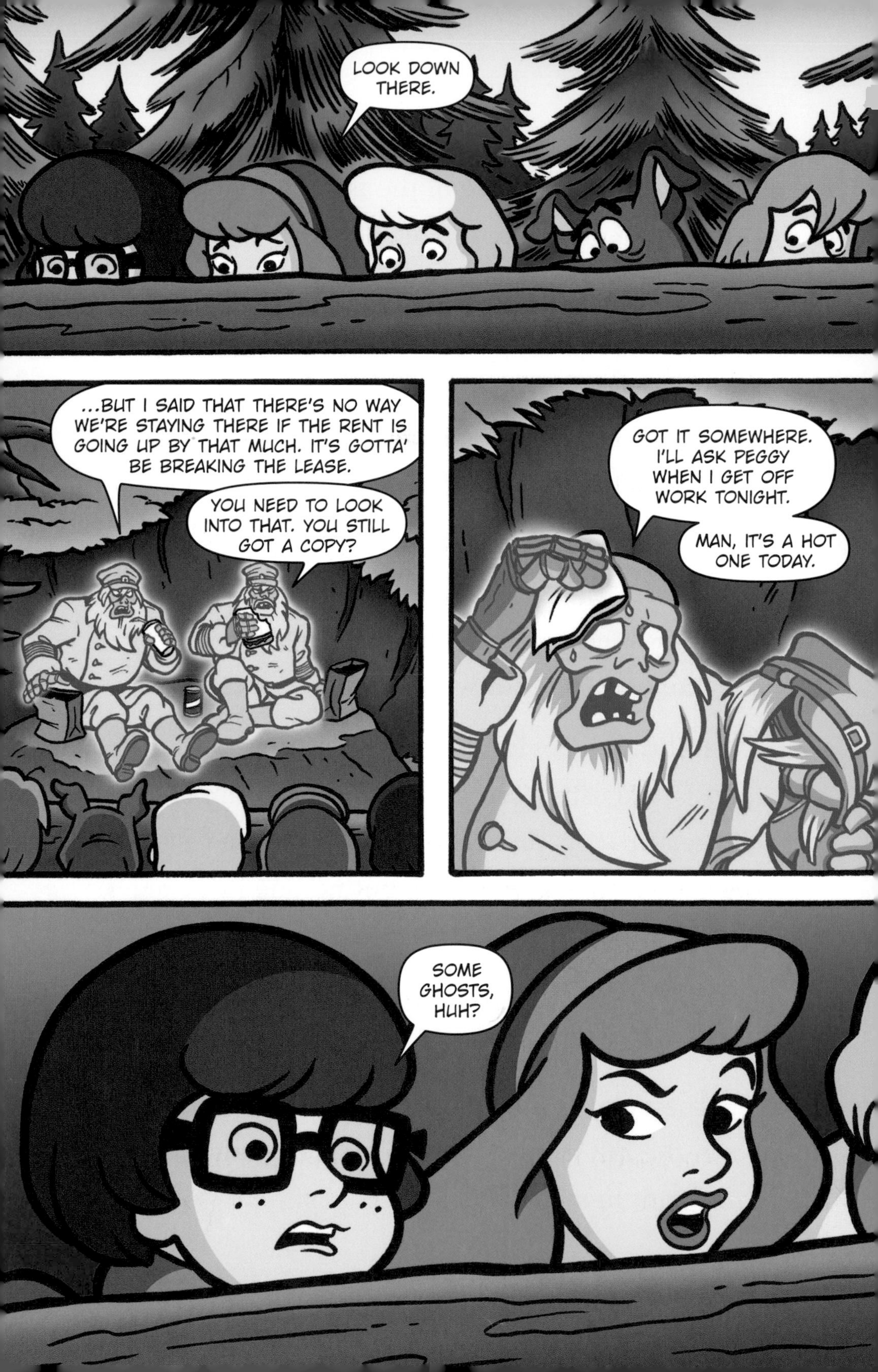
LOOK DOWN THERE.
...BUT I SAID THAT THERE'S NO WAY WE'RE STAYING THERE IF THE RENT IS GOING UP BY THAT MUCH. IT'S GOTTA' BE BREAKING THE LEASE.
YOU NEED TO LOOK INTO THAT. YOU STILL GOT A COPY?
GOT IT SOMEWHERE. I'LL ASK PEGGY WHEN I GET OFF WORK TONIGHT.
MAN, IT'S A HOT ONE TODAY.
SOME GHOSTS, HUH?

The Mystery Inc. gang stayed there, crouched behind a fallen tree trunk for five minutes, just watching the Civil War ghosts. For the most part, they remained quiet. Only Shaggy and Scooby-Doo's constantly growling stomachs broke the silence.

"Hey, guys!" a voice sounded from the other side of the hill.

Shaggy felt a chill run down his spine. But then he realized the shout wasn't directed at his friends. Someone was yelling at the fake ghosts. The gang watched as the two men stood up. They dusted themselves off, collected their trash, and walked over the nearby hill.

When the ghosts had completely disappeared from view, Fred said, "Come on!"

"Did you see those sandwiches, Scoob?" said Shaggy, still thinking about the fake ghosts and their bagged lunches. "I can almost smell the bologna from here."

Scooby-Doo sniffed the air. "Ralami!" he corrected.

"You're right — salami!" said Shaggy, licking his lips. "I'll never doubt your snout again."

"Come on, you two!" Fred repeated.

Against his better instincts, Shaggy followed alongside the gang. They crept around the side of the mountain until they found a nice row of large boulders to duck behind. Shaggy peeked over the rock in front of him. The two fake ghosts were walking down toward a valley far below. A large dump truck was backing up to a massive cave entrance. Inside the truck was a glowing greenish white substance.

"What is that?" asked Daphne, who was peering over the boulder on Shaggy's left.

"Looks like the same stuff we saw in that underground lake," said Fred, standing on Daphne's other side.

"Hey," said Shaggy. "We know that guy!"

The gang looked where Shaggy was pointing. Near the side of the truck stood Mr. Wellcott. It seemed he was instructing the driver on how best to back into the cave entrance.

"This can't be legal," said Velma. "Just look at the side of that truck."

Velma was right, as usual. On the side of the dump truck in large red letters read the words "Hazardous Waste."

"So Mr. Wellcott is the one behind all this," said Fred. "He's hiring people to scare tourists out of the caves."

"So no one stumbles on his illegal dumping," said Velma. "He's covered all his bases."

"He even had his ghosts dress up in the same shade as that . . . that stuff," said Daphne. "Probably in case anyone noticed a weird glowing color while on the tour."

"Speaking of weird glowing ghosts," said Shaggy. "Like, where did those two soldier guys sneak off to?"

Fred and Velma exchanged a look and then peered back over their respective boulders. Shaggy was right. The fake ghosts were nowhere to be found.

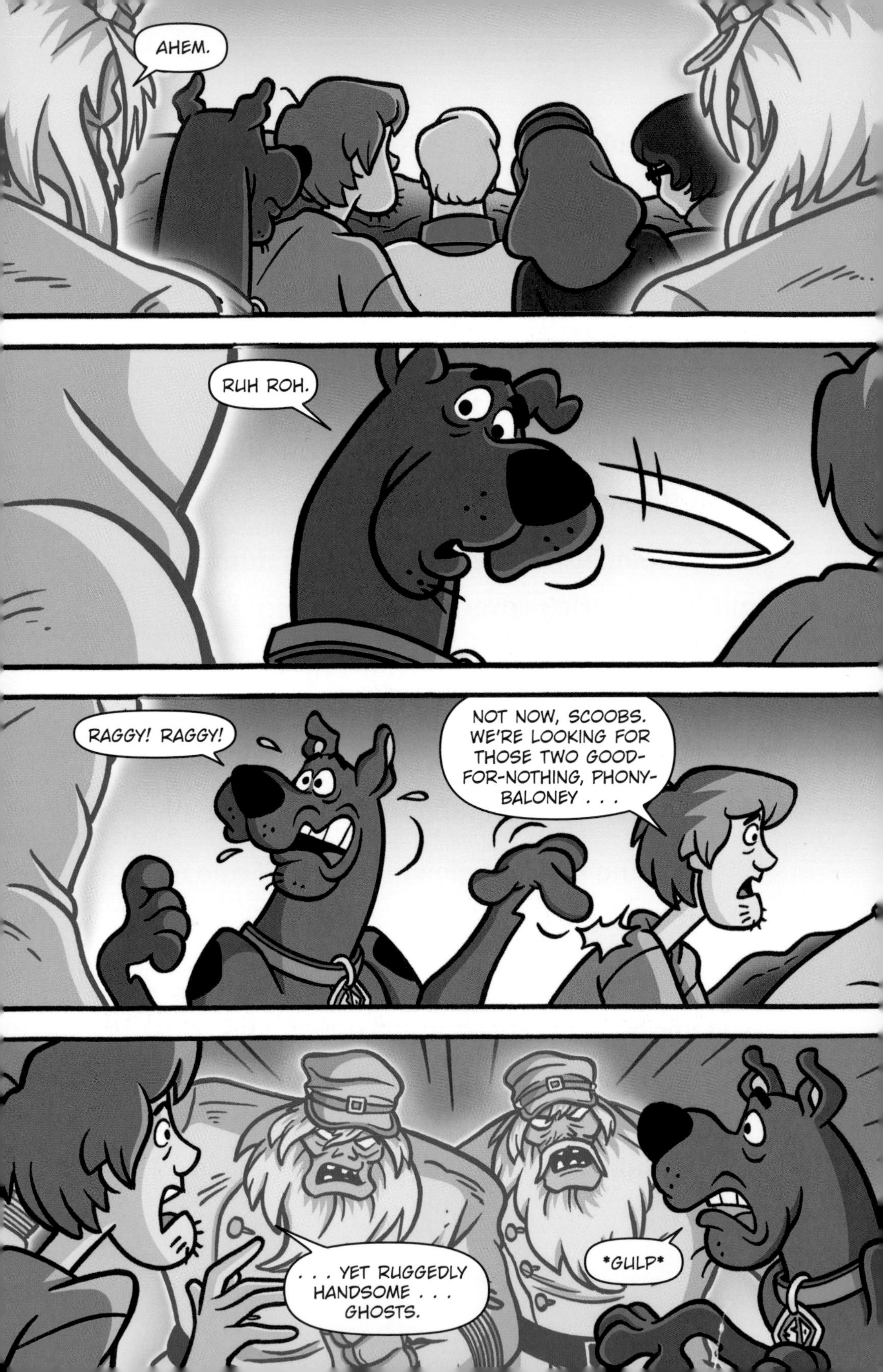
AHEM.
RUH ROH.
RAGGY! RAGGY!
NOT NOW, SCOOBS. WE'RE LOOKING FOR THOSE TWO GOOD-FOR-NOTHING, PHONY-BALONEY . . .
. . . YET RUGGEDLY HANDSOME . . . GHOSTS.
GULP

All the members of the Mystery Incorporated gang were sure that the two Civil War ghost soldiers standing behind them were not the least bit authentic. They were not from the Civil War. They were not soldiers.

They certainly weren't ghosts.

Knowing that information didn't change the fact that they were two large, intimidating men, hired by a criminal mastermind. The truth didn't make anything better. These two men were still quite terrifying.

Scooby-Doo opened his mouth. "R-r-r-r —" he stuttered.

"Spit it out, Scoob!" shouted Shaggy as the men came closer. "On second thought, don't do that!" He shielded himself, remembering his slobber-covered face from earlier that day.

"R-r-r-r —" Scooby continued until he finally got out the word. "RUN!!"

A quick glance to their left and then to their right, Scooby and Shaggy knew that saying anything at that moment was pointless.

The other members of the Mystery Inc. gang had already taken off back down the side of the mountain.

"Like, hey!" shouted Shaggy. "Wait for us!"

"Reh! Rait ror rus!" Scooby repeated.

FWOOOOOOOOOSH!

Shaggy and Scooby-Doo's legs spun like pinwheels. They sped away from the strange men and quickly caught up with their friends.

"They're too fast!" shouted Velma as Shaggy ran past her down the steep slope. "We'll never make it to the Mystery Machine!"

Shaggy looked back over his shoulder. Velma was right. The men were only a few yards behind them. They seemed to be gaining ground with every step.

"Here!" Fred called from further down the hill. Shaggy watched as his friend jumped down into the hole he'd unwittingly discovered earlier.

Daphne quickly followed, as did Velma, and even Scooby-Doo.

Shaggy didn't have much time to think about it one way or the other. He barely had time to even sigh before he followed his friends down into the dark hole.

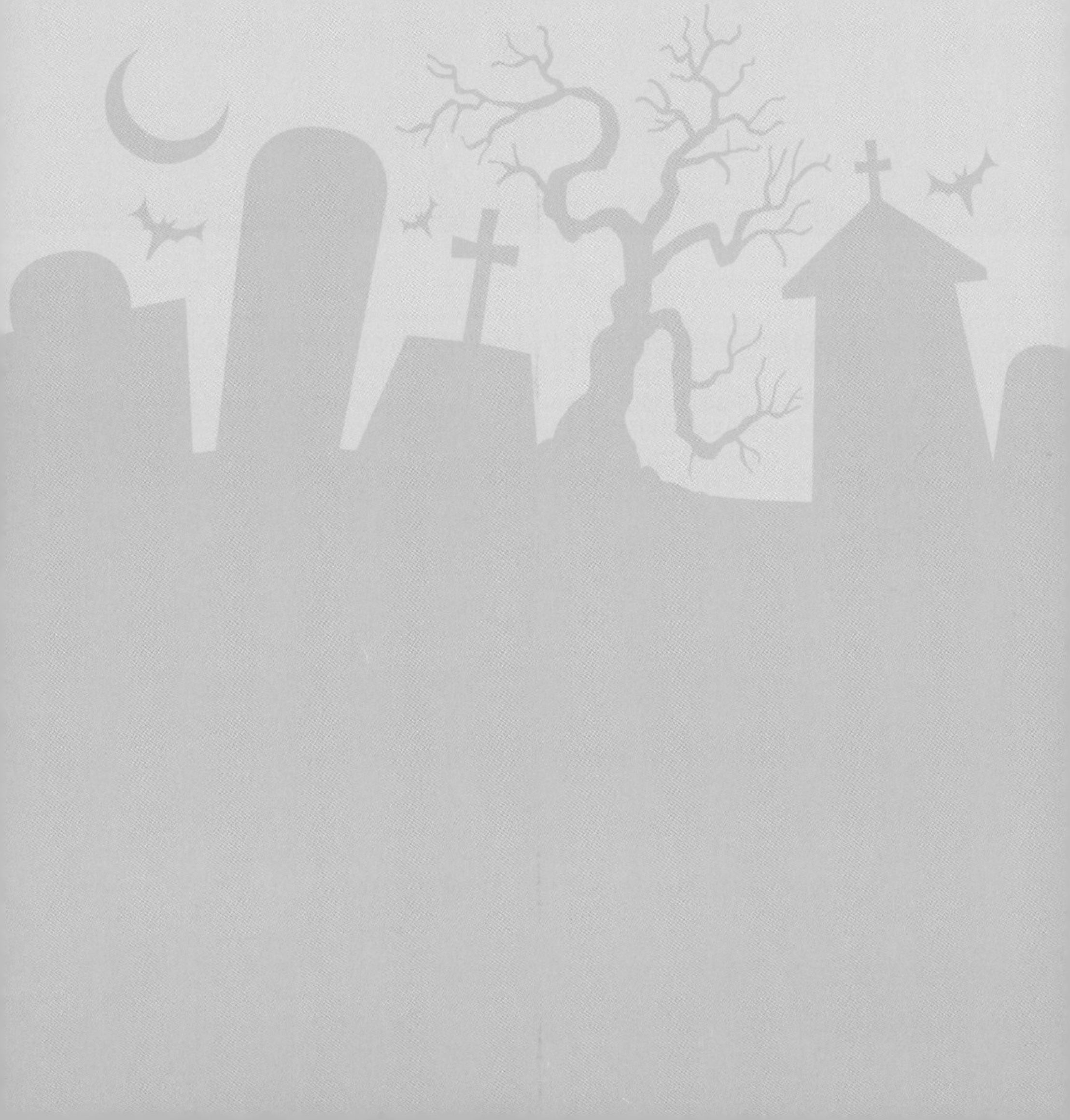

CHAPTER 5

MEDDLING KIDS

WHUMP!

Scooby-Doo and the Mystery Inc. gang landed in a tunnel near the cave entrance.

The entrance to the cave was smaller than Fred had remembered. Once he reached the bottom of the hole, he had to get onto his hands and knees just to crawl through the small opening. He moved as quickly as he could. Even still, he barely avoided Daphne jumping down right on top of him.

The tunnel in front of him was narrow and dark. Fred kept crawling. This was the gang's one chance to get away from those fake ghosts. Fred just had to hope that this passageway joined up with the rest of the cave system.

Fred could hear his friends behind him. He really hoped he wasn't leading them all into a dead end. With every few feet he crawled, he felt better about his decision. The tunnel was getting larger. It wasn't long before Fred could get to his feet. Not long after that, he could stop hunching over completely. Fred breathed a sigh of relief. There were lights up ahead.

* * *

Shaggy didn't share Fred's outlook. From his position in the back of the line, he only cared about putting as much distance between himself and the ghost soldiers as possible. At the moment, that was only a few feet.

About thirty seconds after Shaggy ducked down into the tunnel, he had heard the soldiers jump down into the hole after him.

As he scrambled through the small opening, he'd felt a hand grasp at his pant leg. Shaggy had managed to kick it off, but he knew the men were still on his heels. As he crawled through the tunnel now, he could see the glow from their greenish white body paint illuminate the narrow cave behind him.

As soon as Shaggy could get to his feet, he began to sprint. He didn't care that he couldn't see anything in front of him. He was more worried about what was behind him. He managed to catch up to Scooby-Doo, and the two kept up a fast, even pace. After a few near collisions with cave walls that had no business being where they were, Shaggy saw a faint light in front of him. It wasn't the eerie greenish white glow of the soldiers. It was the warm yellow light of one of the electric lanterns mounted on the cave wall near the tour's path.

But Shaggy didn't have a chance to relax. In fact, he lost his breath completely when he felt a hand on his shoulder.

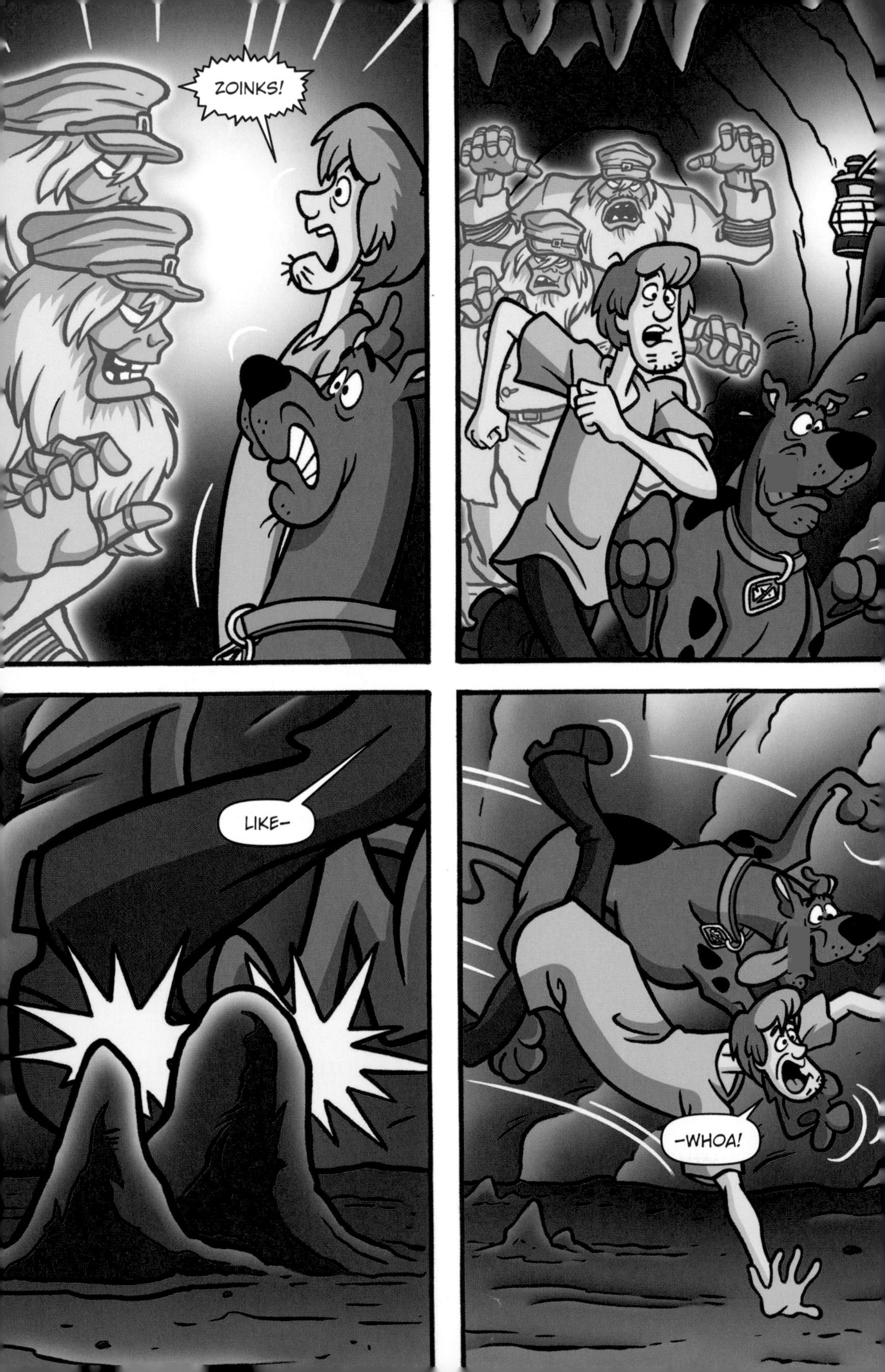
ZOINKS!
LIKE–
–WHOA!

WHUMP!

Scooby-Doo and Shaggy hit the ground — hard.

Shaggy wasn't sure if he'd tripped Scooby or if Scooby-Doo had tripped him. Either way, the two were rolling, more than running, away from the ghost soldiers at the moment. The fake ghosts were right behind them!

Shaggy knew he didn't have a second to waste. As he and Scooby came to a stop on the cave floor, they tried to get right back up on their feet.

They would have, too, if the soldiers weren't so fast. But since the men were following Scooby and Shaggy closely, the pair of criminals had no choice but to trip over them.

The two fake ghosts floundered through the air for a second or two, before coming to a splashing halt in the small stream that ran next to the main cave path.

SPA-LOOOSH!

Shaggy stood up, and offered a hand to Scooby-Doo. After helping his pal back to his paws, Shaggy glanced over at the two ghost soldiers, still lying in a heap in the creek. The greenish white paint that covered their bodies and clothing was slowly running off into the dirty water.

"That doesn't even look real," came a high-pitched voice from a nearby tunnel.

Standing just a few feet away from Scooby and Shaggy was the latest tour group to enter the Linville Caverns. Simon was once again leading the tour. His face seemed even more surprised than the seven or eight tourists standing directly behind him.

A little boy was looking up at his mother with a disappointed expression. "These effects are terrible, Mom," he said.

"No refunds," Simon told the tourists, sounding annoyed. "Your tickets clearly state that we are not responsible for lost or stolen goods, injuries, or fake-looking ghosts."

The little boy's mother checked the fine print on the back of her ticket. "He's right," she said, surprised. "The tickets really say that!"

The little boy frowned.

SPLISH! SPA-LOOOSH!

Shaggy looked at the two "ghosts" again. They were splashing in the creek, trying to get up. Shaggy wondered for a brief second if they were going to run back into the cave system. But the two just sat there, letting the water wash away their glowing paint.

"We almost got away with it," one of the crooks muttered to the other.

"If it weren't for those meddling kids!" the other added.

"Or maybe if you would've used waterproof paint," Shaggy suggested to them.

"Reah," Scooby agreed. "Raterproof raint!"

The two crooks growled and tried to stand again. They slipped on the rocky creek bed and fell back into the water.

SPLOOSH!

"Heehee!" the little boy laughed at that.

Maybe the tour was worth the price of admission after all.

***

"Yep. It was hazardous materials all right," said the sheriff to the Mystery Incorporated gang as they all stood in the parking lot outside the Linville Diner. "We had Gladys show us the way. You all meet Gladys?"

"Creepy old lady in a hood who has a way of disappearing right in front of your eyes?" Shaggy said.

"That's her," said the sheriff.

"Never met her," said Shaggy. He smiled at Scooby-Doo. The sheriff didn't seem to enjoy their particular sense of humor.

"Anyway, Gladys lives up in the hills. Showed us right to the spot Wellcott had been dumping his waste," said the sheriff. "We rounded him up already. Guess there was something to Gladys's ghost stories after all, even if she didn't connect all the dots."

"Thanks for your help," said Velma. She wiped her forehead with her sleeve. The sun was relentless today.

"Guess we'll be on our way. I think we've seen enough cave spirits and caverns with bottomless pits for one day."

"You guys excited to get back in the air-conditioned van?" Fred said, as he pulled the keys to the Mystery Machine out of his pocket. Then he furrowed his brow. Scooby and Shaggy had disappeared. "Guys?" Fred said. He seemed concerned. "Guys!?!"

Daphne put her hand on Fred's shoulder. "Don't worry. They're right there," she said, pointing toward one of the diner's windows.

Through the window, Fred could see Shaggy and Scooby ordering two plates of pancakes. Shaggy was holding his arms as far apart as they could go, in order to indicate how big of a stack he wanted.

"I think we're going to have to deal with a couple more bottomless pits," Velma said.

Fred smiled and then headed toward the diner with Daphne and Velma. Right about now, pancakes didn't seem like a bad idea at all.

BIOGRAPHIES

MATTHEW K. MANNING is the author of the Amazon best-selling hardcover *Batman: A Visual History.* He has contributed to many comic books, including *Beware the Batman, Spider-Man Unlimited, Pirates of the Caribbean: Six Sea Shanties, Justice League Adventures, Looney Tunes,* and *Scooby-Doo, Where Are You?* When not writing comics themselves, Manning often authors books about comics, as well as a series of young-reader books starring Superman, Batman, and the Flash. He currently resides in Asheville, North Carolina, with his wife Dorothy and their two daughters, Lillian and Gwendolyn.

SCOTT NEELY has been a professional illustrator and designer for many years. Since 1999, he's been an official Scooby-Doo and Cartoon Network artist, working on such licensed properties as *Dexter's Laboratory, Johnny Bravo, Courage the Cowardly Dog, Powerpuff Girls,* and more. He has also worked on *Pokémon, Mickey Mouse Clubhouse, My Friends Tigger & Pooh, Handy Manny, Strawberry Shortcake, Bratz,* and many other popular characters. He lives in a suburb of Philadelphia.

COMIC TERMS

caption (KAP-shuhn)—words that appear in a box; captions are often used to set the scene

gutter (GUHT-er)—the space between panels or pages

motion lines (MOH-shuhn LINES)—illustrator-created marks that help show movement in art

panel (PAN-uhl)—a single drawing that has borders around it; each panel is a separate scene on a spread

SFX (ESS-EFF-EKS)—short for sound effects; sound effects are words used to show sounds that occur in the art of a comic

splash (SPLASH)—a large illustration that often covers a full page or more

spread (SPRED)—two side-by-side pages in a comic book

word balloon (WURD BUH-loon)—a speech indicator that includes a character's dialogue or thoughts; a word balloon's tail leads to the speaking character's mouth

GLOSSARY

credible (KRED-uh-buhl)—trustworthy; worthy of being believed

Civil War (SIV-il WOR)—the war between the Southern states and Northern states, from 1861 to 1865

hazardous waste (HAZ-ur-duhss WAYST)— dangerous materials that need to be disposed of safely

idle (EYE-duhl)—not busy, or not working

illuminate (i-LOO-muh-nate)—to light something up, such as a room

random (RAN-duhm)—without any order or purpose

souvenir (soo-vuh-NIHR)—an object kept as a reminder of a person, place, or event

spirit (SPIHR-it)—another name for a ghost

VISUAL QUESTIONS

1. Describe what is happening in this panel from page 70. What clues from the story led you to that conclusion?

2. Describe the differences in these two panels from page 13. How do those differences help tell the story?

3. Illustrators draw motion lines to help show movement in art. In this panel (page 62), what do the arcing lines beside Scooby-Doo's head tell you about his action? Can you find other motion lines in this book's comic panels?

4. Illustrators sometimes use symbols to show emotions or actions in a panel. This panel from page 62 has a couple different symbols: the beads of sweat near Scooby's head and the yellow burst on Shaggy's shoulder. What do you think these symbols mean? Explain.

SCOOBY-DOO JOKES!

Why is the Mystery Inc. gang always so tired on April 1st?
Because they just finished a march of 31 days!

I have to go to the dentist today.

What time?

Tooth-hurty!

What stays in one corner but travels around the world?
A stamp!

I hate to go outside when it's raining cats and dogs.

Don't worry, as long as it doesn't reindeer!

What is the smartest country?
Albania. It has three A's and one B!

What do little bees like to chew?
Bumble gum.

FIND MORE SCOOBY-DOO JOKES IN...

ALSO FROM CAPSTONE!

DISCOVER MORE SCOOBY-DOO COMIC CHAPTER BOOKS!

"Did someone say jewel?" Professor Dinkley exclaimed from the other side of the dig site.

Shaggy pulled the object out of the ground and held it up in the sunlight. He cleaned off the clinging soil. Everyone gasped in surprise.

"It's a ruby!" the professor exclaimed.

"It certainly looks like one," Velma said.

"Do you know what this means, kids?" Dinkley asked excitedly.

"Yeah! Treasure!" Shaggy proclaimed.

"This discovery makes the dig site more important than ever," Professor Dinkley said.

"It also makes it a lot more valuable," Velma observed.

"Maybe the Gator Man is trying to protect the treasure," Shaggy said.

"Or trying to scare people away from it," Daphne replied.

Meanwhile, Fred studied the palm trees growing at the edge of the dig site. He had an idea of how to use them to trap the Gator Man.

56

Belastic's desk, I saw a delivery note about a dozen cupcakes to be delivered to his dressing room," explained Velma. "I knew that any place with cupcakes was the most likely place to find you!"

Shaggy flushed. "Like, this was definitely the first place we looked," he said. "And we certainly only ate real food today. Right, Scoob?"

CHOMP! CHOMP! CHOMP! CHOMP!

Scooby wiped frosting from his mouth. "Reah," he agreed. "Ro rakeup?"

"What did he say?" asked Daphne.

"Never mind," said Shaggy, embarrassed.

62

Once in hallway at was small by the front window. The window looked onto Main Street. But at the moment, it just looked out onto a sea of fog.

Shaggy walked up to the desk and smacked the small bell with his palm.

BRRRING!

Nothing happened.

He looked back at Daphne, who was standing behind him. "Some service, huh?"

"Just be patient, Shaggy," she said.

"Tell that to my stomach," he said, as he turned back around. "Zoinks!" The concierge was standing behind the desk all of the sudden.

"May I help you?" the thin man muttered.

"L-like, we have a reservation?" Shaggy replied. It came out more like a question.

"Of course," the concierge said. He typed something into the computer in front of him.

15

SCOOBY-DOO!
COMIC CHAPTER BOOKS

CURSE OF THE STAGE FRIGHT

12 PAGES OF COMIC ACTION IN EACH BOOK!

SCOOBY-DOO!
COMIC CHAPTER BOOKS

LEGEND OF THE GATOR MAN

12 PAGES OF COMIC ACTION IN EACH BOOK!

SCOOBY-DOO!
COMIC CHAPTER BOOKS

MYSTERY OF THE MIST MONSTER

12 PAGES OF COMIC ACTION IN EACH BOOK!

Discover more at
WWW.CAPSTONEKIDS.COM

Find cool websites and more
books like this one at

WWW.FACTHOUND.COM
Just type in the
BOOK ID: *9781496535856*
and you're ready to go!